The Ballad of Evinrude and Eulalie

The Ballad of Evinrude and Eulalie

Michael S. Atkinson

Table of Contents

1: The Death of Lady Eulalie

I t was quiet in the countryside, but then Evinrude, Crown Prince of the kingdom of Loventry, lived in a quiet age. There weren't the distant wails of police sirens. There weren't train horns or bicycle bells, nor the constant sea-like roar of cars on the interstate racing away to parts unknown. Evinrude didn't even miss these things, since he didn't know about them. All Evinrude could hear as he stared out into the mass green of the forest trees was the occasional distant hooting of a lonely owl. That was it: just long stretches of painful silence, broken only by a faint *hoo*.

He should've been back at the castle, he knew. But Evinrude needed to think. His life had gotten suddenly complicated, and he had to take a minute and sort it out. So he had ridden off alone into the countryside forest near his castle, leaving behind his outraged attendants and courtiers. Princes usually didn't go away on nighttime rides into the woods by themselves. It wasn't responsible. But Evinrude had outright ignored them and taken off. He figured, after all, that he was the Crown Prince, the rightful heir to the throne of Loventry. Being a prince, he could therefore do princely things, like take long vacations at his family's castle, Charmingfell, or go off by himself into the woods to think. What could go wrong?

He certainly had a lot to think about. For one, his prime minister had just died. The prince wasn't terribly broken up; the man was dull as ditchwater, all business, and had never said a comradely word to Evinrude in his life. He had been a capable administrator, though, and now Evinrude was stuck with finding a replacement. Worse, if he wasn't successful in doing so, he might have to rule the country himself. His parents had long since passed, but Evinrude had successfully held off his own coronation as king on the grounds that the prime minister was handling things well enough. Now that the poor old boy was gone, Evinrude had no excuses. Princes, even Crown Princes, could get away with a lot; kings, on the other hand, couldn't. They had responsibilities. That was a word that sent shudders up Evinrude's spine.

His second problem involved love. Even worse, it involved politics, which made for a ghastly combination. Evinrude belonged to House Charming, which had held on to the Loventrian throne for generations thanks to a lot of political maneuvering and a well-placed marriage now and then. As part of this latter policy, Evinrude had been set up with Lady Amaryllis of House Marian, a match arranged by his parents before their deaths. House Marian had a significant treasury and a large number of knights sworn to their banner. His parents' hope had been that by combining Marian's strength with House Charming, Charming's hold on the crown would be secure forever.

Evinrude and Amaryllis would have to do their part in producing heirs, but even so, that shouldn't have been a problem. Evinrude had met Amaryllis on a few formal occasions, and she was all right in the looks department. The prime minister had done his best to administer things until Evinrude was of age, and now he was gone. All seemed well settled for Evinrude to step in, get married, and take over.

Unfortunately, romance had intervened. Evinrude had begun corresponding with a certain Lady Eulalie, whose family ruled and had taken their name from Isle Turtledove. She had attended a Christmas ball the previous year, they'd danced, one thing led to another, and so they had begun writing. Evinrude liked her. He liked her a lot more than Amaryllis, whom he hardly even knew. On the other hand, he knew disastrous things could happen when a prince abandoned a commitment to marry someone in order to marry someone else. House Turtledove didn't have many sworn banners, and its finances were reportedly gloomy. Worse, although no one spoke of it openly, House Charming's personal treasury was running short. He needed House Marian's fortune to back up his claim to the throne, now that it really looked like he would have to rule. It was a vexing dilemma.

Then, as he wandered about haphazardly on the forest path, he heard a flutter of wings. It didn't sound like the distant owl. It sounded like a messenger bird. That meant trouble. Messenger birds late at night always meant trouble.

Evinrude pulled up his horse and waited on the path. He had found in his experience that it was much more efficient to wait for messenger birds to find him than to go out searching in an attempt to find them. Sure enough, through the trees a bedraggled raven came fluttering. It dropped a scroll into his outstretched hand, squawked indignantly at him, and then flew away again.

Evinrude unrolled the scroll and read swiftly. The message was a mere three sentences. *A dragon has attacked Isle Turtledove. Eulalie is missing. Send help.*

The Crown Prince reached for his sword, spurred his horse into a gallop and raced away, back towards the castle. Life was no longer complicated. He no longer had thoughts about Amaryllis; indeed, he had only one thought now. He was going to Isle Turtledove as fast as he could, he was going to find Eulalie, and if she could not be found, he was going to find the dragon responsible.

Lady Eulalie had been sitting on the beach when the dragon came. It was a blazing sunny day, perfect for beach-sitting. Isle Turtledove had a fair number of beaches; Eulalie, being who she was, had her own private one. It was a nice little beach, with a view of the channel between the island and the mainland, which meant it was sheltered from the occasional storm that blew in from the sea. The pathway to it was guarded by castle soldiers, so she thought she was safe in going there alone. She had been gazing happily out at the blue-green waters of the channel when a shadow passed over her head. At first, she thought it was a cloud. Then the cloud dived.

She didn't have time to run or call for help. The dragon, scales gleaming, massive bat-like wings tearing at the air, thundered down and slammed to the beach in a spray of sand and smoke. Eulalie screamed, expecting to burn in seconds.

Then the dragon paused. "Oh, blast," it rumbled. "This isn't right. This isn't right at all."

"I beg your pardon?" Eulalie said shakily.

"You're alone," the dragon said. "I can't flame you if you're alone. It's not fair."

"It's not… fair," she repeated.

"No. You're supposed to be protected by a knight. I flame him, and then I flame you. Gives you a sporting chance, you see."

Eulalie considered herself to be an expert on matters of etiquette. This one was completely new to her. "I didn't realize that there were rules for this sort of thing."

The dragon drew itself up, looking offended. "There are indeed. We are *civilized* dragons. We don't just fly about where we please, burn people, and steal their treasure. We're organized. We have standards. We have *contracts*. We do honest work for honest treasure."

"You mean you're paid for this?" Eulalie said.

"Of course," the dragon said, a little condescendingly. Eulalie had never before been condescended to by a dragon. "Those big mountain caves don't pay for themselves, you know. There are property taxes to consider, and enchantment fees, and scale repair costs."

"Oh," said Eulalie. "So… someone paid you to come and attack me."

"Exactly," the dragon said. "But there are expectations in return. The client was clearly informed. I can't attack you if you're undefended." It glared at her, as if it was her fault for messing up what should have been a neat and tidy job.

"I'm so sorry," Eulalie said. "If you like, I'll go and fetch help. My castle is just down the road. There's a few soldiers there. They can give you a good fight, I'm sure of it."

"Well, that's the thing…" the dragon rumbled. "The point of the contract is there has to be a successful flaming. If I let you leave and you summon your soldiers, they might actually drive me off with arrows or magic or something else. No, I'm afraid I'll have to make an exception and flame you now. The client will have to understand, given the circumstances."

"You don't have to do that!" Eulalie pleaded desperately. "I promise, I won't call a whole army, I've only got just a few knights. I'd only call one of them, I promise. I've got the perfect man in mind, his name's Smith, he's got a wooden leg, you won't have any trouble at all!"

"Sorry," said the dragon, "but there's no help for it. I do feel badly about all this."

"Oh, stuff it," Eulalie snapped. Then she saw the dragon opening its jaws. She gasped.

"Wait," she tried once more, desperate, "I'm not prepared, I'm not dressed properly, I'm only wearing this light thing, and I left my special lucky corset in my room, my mother made it for me, it's whalebone, she made it herself, if you just let me go and get it, I'll come right back!"

"No, you won't," the dragon said tiredly. "Now, look, I'm going to go ahead and flame, all right? Again, I am sorry."

She was out of ideas. She looked for a weapon she could use, but there was nothing to hand. It wouldn't have been of help even if she had one; Eulalie had never trained in the military arts; she had read about them and had thought about it, but had never gotten around to actual practice. Now here she was, in her last seconds of life, about to be flamed by a dragon, and she could see no way out.

Eulalie wanted something more appropriate for her last words than going on about her corset, at least. Then she realized that no one would ever know the difference anyway. She took a breath and unleashed a torrent of the most dreadful language she knew, things sailors shouted in the docks. Everyone at court would have been scandalized. She was still screaming insults as the dragon flamed.

The proprietor of the White Beetle Inn on Kirtle Island had a mania for neatness, and he just hated dingy smoke-filled rooms where all sorts of unsavory people could meet and conduct transactions of questionable legality. So not only had he built his inn with an abundance of windows and lanterns, flooding the place with light, he'd also constructed his fireplaces so as to create a minimum of smoke. He had even arranged for a constable to sit by the bar and keep an eye on things. The White Beetle was, as a result, perfectly respectable, and so were its customers.

Rowena, member of the magical Order of the Rabbit, was a customer who appeared definitely respectable. She was known to use her magic to make sure that the winds and waves were favorable, and provide direction for sailors with faulty maps. Evinrude, being the Prince of House Charming, was also respectable. No one could have found any fault with their meeting at the White Beetle. What Evinrude wanted, however, was out of Rowena's usual line of work.

"I need to find a dragon."

"You what?" said Rowena.

"Dragon," Evinrude repeated. "I need to find it."

Rowena paused. Could this be a trick by someone trying to find her out? "My dear sir, why on Earth would you-"

She hadn't noticed the glass vial of light grey ash he was carrying. Now he drew it out and set it before her with a clunk of cold finality. "This used to be a friend of mine. She got flamed. I want to find who did it."

"I see," said Rowena slowly. "And you'd like me to sense where the dragon is?"

"Yes. And who hired him," Evinrude said. "I know how these things are. Dragons these days work under contract. After I kill the dragon, I'm going after whoever sent him."

"Oh," Rowena said. "That might be more complicated. The wizard would be several removes away from the, ah, remains, and-"

"Can you do it?" Evinrude cut in. He didn't snap, or roar, or thunder at her. He just asked, very calmly. But Rowena felt unnerved nonetheless.

"I can try," she said at last. She was still suspicious, but it wouldn't hurt to check it out. Rowena took her wand, tapped the vial, and closed her eyes. One of the basic rules of magic was that if you killed or were killed by something magical, a link was created between you and it. Someone like Rowena could trace that link in their minds, as easily as following a line on a map, and find out what had done you in. She did that now.

She could sense the dragon's traces lingering around the vial; it left an acrid, burning feeling in her mind. Rowena, eyes closed, followed the link. A golden beach flashed in her mind, then a long running coastline, then the cold waters of a distant inlet. She saw a cave overlooking the narrow water and stars above the cave. Rowena carefully noted the positions of those stars.

"Right," she said, still with her eyes closed. "I know where the dragon is."

"Wonderful," Evinrude said. "What about who sent him?

"Hang on," Rowena said irritably. "This isn't easy work, you know."

She concentrated again, seeing the cave in her mind. She had a lock on the dragon's thread now, and that meant she might be able to find the wizard who had summoned the dragon. She followed the dragon's mystical thread around the cave until a darker thread lit in her mind, a thread twisting and powerful. She gasped. Rowena knew that magical signature, knew it like her own hand. It was Mortimer, a known dark wizard of the Order of the Polecat, a mercenary who would summon dragons for the highest bidder and who had no ethics whatsoever. He was also her father.

She had taken great pains to cover that up. No one on Kirtle Island knew. Her fellow Rabbits didn't know. She'd broken off a marriage, abandoned her family, invented a whole new identity, even committed the foulest of crimes, just to cover her tracks. So far she'd managed to keep it all quiet, mostly because she had stayed on her island and caused no trouble. Her secret should've been kept securely for life.

However, if she sent Evinrude after the dragon now and he confronted Mortimer, he might find out. She could tell by his intensity that he wouldn't let it go. Rowena decided that he couldn't find out.

"You'll have to keep sailing due west from here for twenty days," she said. "On the twenty-first day you will come to an extinct volcano. Inside the volcano's cone you will find the dragon and the wizard who sent him."

"Thanks," said Evinrude, and without ceremony he took back the vial, laid some gold before her, and walked away. Rowena sighed. The volcano existed; that was true. It was also a home of a giant of fearsome reputation, one who generally lay asleep and who absolutely did not like to be disturbed. Once Evinrude stepped on the island, Rowena knew she would never see him again. All the same, she didn't sleep particularly well that night.

Evinrude had never before seen black sand. The volcanic cone of the island towered ominously above him, and threatening rumbles shook the ground on which he stood. Still, he was almost happy. After twenty days of sailing, he had finally reached the island.

His ship had dropped anchor just moments before. Evinrude was the only one on the beach. The captain had offered to send soldiers with him and had even volunteered to accompany the Prince himself. Evinrude had turned down the offer. "I'm doing this alone," he said. "Just me and the dragon. No one else." Then he leapt ashore and marched bravely off into the nearest cave, certain that it was where the dragon lay.

As Evinrude approached the cave cautiously, he expected to feel a blast of hot air against his face. He had of course heard of dragon caves, heard of their notorious treasure hoards, heard of the burglars that occasionally attempted to make off with some of the smaller shiny bits. He had also heard that dragons usually lay about their caves, snoring and breathing fire. He was therefore surprised when he found the cave dark and cold, littered about with bones, torches guttering dull and red on the walls. He heard a distant rumble that didn't quite sound like the roaring of a dragon.

Evinrude began to wonder if this cave might actually belong to someone or something else. He hesitated for a moment, and then took one cautious step forward.

Outside, the crew was beginning to get nervous. The captain, mindful of Evinrude's orders, waited for an appropriate period of time. Finally, he decided enough was enough. He ordered two soldiers to grab their swords and follow him, and they started for the cave.

The captain and his men had just made it inside when they saw Evinrude dashing towards them, eyes wide with alarm. Behind the prince lurched a gigantic figure, roaring loudly and waving its massive arms, shaking the very ground with every step. Then Evinrude tripped. The giant charged upon him. The captain, his soldiers following, bolted back to the ship. He looked back once. Evinrude wasn't behind him.

The crew was greatly dismayed at the news, but the captain headed off a rescue by describing the giant in all its size and strength, and then point-blank ordered them away. The crew prudently didn't object.

Rowena woke up from a disturbed sleep. Someone was banging on her door. She could tell by the grey light filtering in through her windows that it was just barely morning. She stumbled to the door, yawning. "I'm sorry," she said as she pulled it open, "but I only offer assistance between the hours of eight and five-"

The man was short and his clothes smudged. He smelled like he had been in a quarrel with a trash bin and lost. To Rowena's senses, he smelled dirty in more ways than one; his magical power guttered around him like a torch thrown into a sewer. She could sense echoes of something else too, acrid and smoky.

"You again," Rowena said, looking around hastily to see if anyone else was about. "You'd better get inside quick, before anyone sees you." She wrinkled her nose distastefully. "Or smells you."

The man gave a hiccup of protest. "I'm a great wizard, and your father; there's no call to be talkin' to me like that!"

"Fine," Rowena said. "I'm sorry. Now will you come in, quickly?"

Mortimer, Order of the Polecat, scurried in, grumbling all the way. "I've summoned dragons, y'know, I ain't to be trifled with, nossir I'm not..."

She drew her wand, conjured up some tea, and shoved it at him. Ordinarily she liked to make it herself, non-magically, but these were desperate circumstances. "Right, then," she said, as Mortimer glared suspiciously at the tea, "What is it this time?"

"Ah. Well, Charlotte, my dear ... I need help."

"Help," she said flatly. "What for? And my name is Rowena now. You should remember that."

Mortimer finally ventured a taste of the tea. It didn't kill him instantly, or turn him into a spotted toad, so he persevered on with it as he talked. "Oh, Rowena, is it? Not the name we gave you. But it's just as well, I suppose. I didn't like Charlotte anyway, I wanted something else, but your mother, well, she insisted...anyway, here it is. I summoned a dragon for a chap recently, and it seems he, the fella, not the dragon, doesn't like me hangin' round. I'm a loose end, y'know."

Cold fear shot through Rowena. "Your employer is coming after you."

"You've got it now. There I was, mindin' my own business, lying around on the beach, takin' in the sea, when I was attacked!"

"By…"

"By a lizard," Mortimer said impressively.

"A lizard."

"Yes."

"A fire-breathing lizard?"

"Well, no, not as such…"

"A giant lizard, magically enlarged to the size of a bear?" Rowena asked.

"No, it was about the usual size…"

"A deadly poisonous lizard, perhaps?"

"It might've been!" Mortimer shouted.

"But it wasn't, was it," Rowena said. "Father, have you been drinking again? Or, perhaps, did you ever stop?"

Mortimer leaned in close. "Listen, Rowena, I know it's been a while since you've done Polecat work and I know you call yourself a Rabbit now-"

"I *am* a Rabbit now!" Rowena said harshly.

"Fine," Mortimer said, backing off and raising his hands. "Anyway, it's been a while, or maybe you've forgotten, but we Polecats, we don't do things like you Rabbits. That lizard was walkin', right out in the open, in a crowded establishment (I won't say what kind), walkin' right towards me. Lizards usually scuttle away, don't they? Not this one. This lizard meant business. My employer's gone and hired another Polecat to come after me. Typical."

Rowena should've called the authorities. She would have, had he been anyone else or had she not had reasons of her own to keep quiet. "Fine. I have a cloak of disguise. It's in the closet there."

Mortimer hesitated. "You don't have an invisibility cloak by any chance?"

"Invisibility's overrated," Rowena said curtly. "Useless in rain, snow, crowds, and mud. Disguise works better. People just don't notice you. They look past you, mistake you for someone else, that sort of thing. Anyway, that's all I have. Take it and get to the harbor. There's a ship heading south. You'll be out of these waters in an hour."

Mortimer pledged his thanks and undying gratitude. Rowena didn't believe a word of it. She watched as he struggled into the cloak. Then she turned away. Behind her, she heard rapid footsteps, and then her door slammed. She could only hope he would get away safely. Rowena wondered if she would ever sleep soundly again. All her years of trying to live quietly out of the way as a Rabbit, and now he had to turn up again to complicate matters.

"This," she muttered grimly to herself, "is going to be a problem."

2: The Treachery of Lord Philip

Lady Amaryllis of House Marian had first met Lord Philip of House Shirley at the Faun's Summer Ball in the capital of Loventry in late July. Amaryllis had no idea why the Faun's Summer Ball was called that; she'd never seen any actual fauns there or anywhere else in Loventry. She didn't even want to go; she was pledged to Prince Evinrude and he wasn't going. She was frightfully bored at first, and spent most of the first hour lingering around the punch table. Then Lord Philip asked her to dance.

At first they kept to suitable topics like the weather. They established that it was raining, that it had been raining for a while, and that it was likely to clear up soon, it being summer. That settled, the conversation hit a slight lull. Finally, Amaryllis took a risk and ventured into dangerous territory with a question about politics. She remembered that House Shirley hailed from the southern coast and was very keen on trade. What did Philip think of the prime minister's new tax on coastal shipping routes?

She expected to be dismissed out of hand. This wasn't her first spin around the ballroom floor; she knew that noblemen usually didn't care about the political opinions of a lady. To her surprise, Philip responded with a thoughtful critique of the new taxation policy and suggested several alternatives. Amaryllis, startled, asked whether he thought the alternatives were realistic. Twelve minutes later, they had left economics and dived into foreign policy, as the musicians flailed away at their violins in the corner. It had been the happiest evening of Amaryllis's life.

They next met at Christmas. Amaryllis was marching steadily through the endless round of holiday feasts, balls, and carriage rides, longing for it all to be over. Then came Christmas Eve. House Marian, along with the royal family and most of the other aristocracy on hand in the capital, had packed themselves into the cathedral for the traditional Christmas Eve service. Afterwards, as Amaryllis stepped out into the cold midnight air, she missed her coachman. (It turned out later that he had gone off drinking with a scullery maid.) Philip approached and offered a lift.

Amaryllis accepted gladly, and they spent another lovely hour talking about politics. As they said goodnight at her door, Philip asked hesitantly whether she might visit him down in Shirleyhold, his family's ancestral castle.

"I'm sorry," Amaryllis said, hating what she had to say. "I can't. I'm pledged."

"Who?"

"Evinrude."

"Ah," said Philip, and went away.

She didn't see him again for six months. She met Evinrude once. They talked about the weather.

July came round again. Amaryllis had gone to her country house in the north, tucked away in cool mountain pines. The Faun's Summer Ball was coming up, but she wanted even less to go this year. She wondered if she could feign illness.

Then, the night before the ball, as Amaryllis was settling miserably into her room back in her capital residence, Philip arrived at the door. "I, er, found a letter," he explained hesitantly, once he had been admitted. "You should read it."

It wasn't addressed to her. It was addressed to Lady Eulalie from Isle Turtledove. Amaryllis hesitated, not wishing to read someone else's post. Then she recognized the handwriting and the royal stamp. It was Evinrude's letter, and he was saying some very friendly things to Eulalie, things that were entirely much too friendly.

"How did you get this?" Amaryllis demanded.

"That's not important," Philip said. "Let's just say I know a few wizards who come in helpful at times like this. The point is, he's pledged to you. But he writes more like he's pledged to her."

Amaryllis crumpled the letter in her hand. "I shall have to do something about this."

"The thing is… I already did. "

"What?"

Philip smiled. "We're not just keen on trade, you know. As I mentioned, House Shirley has an acquaintance with certain powerful wizards. We don't talk about it much. People might think it's cheating."

"And so you…"

"I sent a dragon after her. She should be cinders by now. Prince Evinrude has gone away on a futile quest to hunt the dragon down. He's not likely to come back. And since you were pledged to him, and he has no heir and no family…"

Amaryllis swiftly grasped the implications. She smiled brilliantly. "You darling."

What followed made for really the happiest evening of her life.

Lady Amaryllis stood on the grand balcony of Shirleyhold and waved as the griffins thundered overhead. She had never before seen so many. She wondered where Philip had found them all. The last griffin she had seen before today had been an elderly creature named Max, who puttered about the castle garden. Now suddenly Philip had assembled whole flights of griffins, young and strong, clearly eager for battle.

She looked down at the broad parade ground that swept towards the outer wall of the castle. The parade ground filled with mustering soldiers, the cavalry on horseback, the infantry in neat lines ranged in companies beneath the combined banners of House Marian and House Shirley, snapping in the wind. Amaryllis felt the balcony quiver beneath her, just for an instant, and she gasped. A column of dragons had just marched into the parade ground, their massive wings high, jaws agape and spouting flame. Amaryllis, impressed as she was, felt a shiver of fear.

Philip came up beside her. "And so there is our army," he said, or rather shouted, over the thunder of the griffin flights and the ponderous tread of the dragons. "What do you think of it?"

"It's lovely," Amaryllis said, not quite enthusiastically.

Philip noticed her hesitation. "You're not getting nerves now, are you? Not when we're so close?"

It was true. They were nearly where they wanted to be. Lady Eulalie had been flamed by a dragon. Prince Evinrude had gone off to avenge her, but no one had heard from him for weeks. This was not unusual; lone knights weren't nearly as successful against fire-breathing dragons as the stories made out.

Everyone expected Amaryllis to take the throne now. It only made sense; Evinrude had been Crown Prince and had no heirs, Amaryllis had been his betrothed. All that remained was to schedule the coronation. Just in case there were any doubts, however, there was the army.

"No," Amaryllis said. "I'm not balking. You're going to invade Lydwin up north, you'll be a hero in the war, and you'll use that to secure my claim. I assume, of course, that you'll win."

"I will win," Philip assured her, his grey eyes cold with absolute confidence. "Look at the army. And we've got wizards, too. The Lydwinish have more men, maybe, but do they have wizards? No. My people can summon dragons; the Lydwinish can't even enchant a broom to sweep a floor."

"Yes, but…" Amaryllis sighed. "I can't help feeling we've gone awfully far. It's one thing to get rid of Eulalie. That served her right. But a war is serious business. And how will you start it? Lydwin hasn't actually attacked us yet. You can't just storm over the border and expect the other houses to support you. They'll say Shirley and Marian have gone rogue, and they'll support someone more sensible for the crown."

"You're absolutely right, darling," Philip said. He stepped away from the balcony, leaving Amaryllis alone by the rail. "Did I mention that the Lydwinish also have very skilled archers?"

"Archers? What-"

Amaryllis didn't hear the distant twang, not over the thunder of the army. She felt the arrow though, as it slammed into her with such force that she fell back, over the rail, and plummeted down towards the parade ground. She realized the full scope of his treachery two seconds before she smacked hard into the unforgiving parade ground rock.

Philip shouted for help. "The Lady Amaryllis has been cruelly murdered!" His guards rushed to meet his call, and when they reached Amaryllis's body, they found a Lydwinish arrow plain as day. House Marian and House Shirley demanded vengeance, and the other houses, appalled at the violent act, fell in line. Lydwin denied everything, but it didn't really matter. Philip, apparently mad with grief, immediately launched the army. The other houses sent their knights to help. In the chaos of those first few days after Amaryllis' assassination, Philip found his way into assuming the place of Prime Minister. It made sense; he was leading a war, after all. No one dared to object.

The stories often tell of heroic knights who, alone and wielding only their trusty sword and sturdy shield, bravely venture forth to slay the dragon and rescue the damsel in distress. The stories are, of course, bunk. A dragon is a multi-ton flying armored monster with the ability to let loose an inferno of fire that can melt through steel like a knife through butter. An average knight, on his own, stands about as much chance as a snowball in the Infernal Regions. A whole squadron of knights backed by archers, with a lot of hard work and a fair amount of luck, might have a chance, just. If a well-aimed arrow makes a one-in-a-thousand hit into an open spot in the dragon's scales, or stabs it in the eye, then maybe that dragon might be brought down. But when one considers that Philip of House Shirley had unleashed entire flights of hired dragons against the Lydwinish army, and backed them up with more flights of griffins, and an army of fighting men besides, it is no wonder that the new Prime Minister of Loventry felt supremely confident in his war.

He stood in his map room, watching his lines move forward in great leaps across enemy territory. He didn't even notice at first when Rowena materialized in the corner of his room. She had to make a nervous cough in order to get his attention before tucking a sock into a pocket of her robe.

"Ah," Philip said. "I'm curious about the sock."

"Wizard lore," Rowena said. "You don't need to know."

She had long since forgotten the thrill of wonder she had felt the first time she had learned about the Sock Dimension, the mystical between-the-worlds place that all uncared-for socks go when their owners aren't looking. She had even forgotten when she had first read about Dorian the Great, the ancient wizard who had worked out the truth that all socks, wherever they are, maintain a link to the Sock Dimension, and that if a person said the spells right and had a spare sock at the ready, they could jump into the Sock Dimension and from there jump out again into anywhere else a sock has been. As socks have been almost anywhere, this meant one could magically go almost everywhere. Dorian had, by that discovery, revolutionized magical transportation.

"Right," Philip said, who had of course never heard of Dorian. "Anyway, you've arrived. I read your letter. Now explain why I should employ you in the service of House Shirley."

"I'm afraid you'll need to do more than that," Rowena said. "I can see what's coming. You won't stop at being Prime Minister; you'll end up being the king of Loventry. Someone else will be Prime Minister then. That someone will be me."

Philip almost laughed. "You're very ambitious, aren't you?"

"I'm highly motivated," Rowena said, "Which amounts to the same thing."

"And I should make you second in the kingdom because…?"

Rowena stared directly at him. "I know what you did. I know you hired Mortimer of the Polecat Order to summon the dragon that killed Lady Eulalie. I have been to Shirleyhold, and I read the traces there. I know you murdered Lady Amaryllis and used her death as a pretext for invading Lydwin. And I know that if Prince Evinrude were still alive, he would be very upset with you."

There was a slight pause, as Philip noted her use of the past tense.

"But Evinrude is not alive," Philip said.

"No. He is not. Why? Because I sent him to his death."

"*Real*-ly."

Rowena explained how she had misdirected Evinrude. She left out a few key points, primarily the part about Mortimer being her father, but she got the main idea across, which was that Evinrude was most definitely dead now, and it was because of her. "In short," Rowena concluded, "not to put too fine a point on it, you owe me."

"Fair enough," Philip said. "Or, I could just murder you here and now, and no one would ever know." He laid a hand on his sword.

"Yes, you could," Rowena replied calmly. "But I don't think you will. You have a problem, you see. I know you sent someone, most likely a Polecat wizard, to assassinate Mortimer. The assassin may have succeeded; he may not. But if he did, whom will you send to deal with him?"

Philip, clever as he was, hadn't thought of that. "Ah…."

Rowena came to the point. "Make me Prime Minister when you assume the throne, and I will protect you in case your dark wizard friends turn against you. You will also have the support of the Order of the Rabbit in your claim, and that is no small thing."

The Prime Minister, whatever else he was, was not a man of indecision. "Done." He extended his hand. Rowena only stared hard at him.

"I am curious," she said at last. "Why? Why all this?"

Philip shrugged. "I wanted to be king. Evinrude was in my way."

"It's as good a reason as any, I imagine," Rowena said.

Philip became king at the beginning of the winter season, just in time to receive the surrender of the last Lydwinish forces. As promised, Rowena became his Prime Minister. She immediately arranged for a squadron of Philip's men to visit her hometown in force and destroy any records of her birth and family, anything or anyone that could provide evidence that she had ever been linked to Mortimer or his Order. They were extremely thorough.

When Rowena received the word that the job had been done, she allowed herself to relax just a fraction. She was the second-most powerful person in the country now, and no one knew that she was or ever had been connected to the Polecats. Not even Philip knew that. Her secret would be safe forever now. That, of course, had been the whole point.

Evinrude, meanwhile, was wafting through space as a disembodied consciousness. He wasn't entirely sure how this had happened. He had been running for his life down a tunnel as a giant monster charged at him, when quite suddenly he had tripped. Evinrude had expected to be eaten, or possibly stepped on. Then everything had gone black.

He waited, for a while, and nothing changed. Evinrude wondered uneasily if this was the afterlife. Perhaps he had been sent there for his sins. The question was: what were his sins? He'd been the crown prince, not the actual king, so he'd never had a chance to influence his country's policies. The only thing that came to mind was that he'd sent letters bordering on the romantic to Lady Eulalie while he had been betrothed to Lady Amaryllis. All right, Evinrude admitted, that was pretty bad. True, on the few occasions when he had met with his intended, their conversation had never left the topic of the weather. But perhaps that was his fault. Perhaps he should have made more of an effort to understand Amaryllis. His conversations had just been so much easier with Lady Eulalie. Still, he had responsibilities. If he could only get back to Loventry, he vowed, he would fix things.

At that moment, a light shone in the void. The figure resolved itself into a woman, who appeared somewhat stressed. "Oh, okay, you're here. Great. So, who are you, and what do you want?"

"What?" Evinrude said.

"Sorry," she said, pushing back her hair and consulting a flashcard. "I'm new at this. St. Peter used to handle all the incoming arrivals, but there's so *many* now, you know. Constance told me there's eight *billion* on Earth alone now, not to mention all the other worlds, and so naturally you understand why he had to delegate. He's also gotten into films lately, particularly ones by that Dwayne Johnson guy, what with Dwayne being called the Rock in those wrestling matches the humans like (I don't watch myself), and Peter, well, that literally *means* rock in the original Greek, and, well... you know... anyway. My name's Sally."

"I'm Evinrude," he said. "I'm sorry, who are you?"

"Actually, that's my line," Sally said. She consulted her flashcard again. "See, I'm an angel. Sally, fourth class. Anyway, I'm supposed to ask you the question, and then you answer, and then we review your life history, and then you answer again, and then I send you on to your eternal reward. You're supposed to get a moral out of this!" she added helpfully.

"Wait," Evinrude said. "You're an angel. Is this Heaven, then?"

"Well, yes," Sally said. "Oh dear. I kinda thought you'd know that. Um...." She wrung her hands. "Usually there's another angel that does this part..."

"What part?"

"The thing is..." Sally sighed. "You're dead. Like, really dead. You, um, got killed by a giant monster. I forget his name. He's got a mom, too, but that's not important. Funny thing; on Earth there's a cousin or something of his who got killed by some Viking guy. Killed both the giant monster and his mom. Constance thought the story rocked but I think it was awful, you know? I mean, the guy's mom? Anyway, here you are, and as I said before, I'm supposed to send you on to Heaven now, so, yeah. Can we start over?"

Evinrude was still trying to process the fact that he was dead by the hand of a giant, never mind all the rest of it. "Certainly," he said, falling back on his princely training in manners. "As I said, I'm Evinrude, and I used to live in Laffin, the capital of Loventry, and-"

Sally couldn't help it. "I'm sorry," she said, trying to choke back a laugh, "The capital's name is Laffin? You lived in Laffin, Loventry?"

"Yes," Evinrude explained wearily, "We're not sure where the name came from. We think the king who settled the place had a few too many drinks one night and couldn't sober up in time for the naming ceremony. Anyway, it's tradition now, and we're stuck with it. As I was saying…"

"Right," Sally said, "Yes, yes, right. What is it you want?"

"What I really want?" Evinrude said.

"Yes," Sally said. "What you really, really want." She paused. "I'm not sure I have the right card…"

"What I really want," Evinrude said, "is to get back to where I came from."

"Er, that's not quite how it works…" Sally sorted through her cards and attempted to explain again, thinking that perhaps she had not been clear. "See, you're supposed to reflect more deeply, consider your life choices…"

Suddenly she brightened up. "Why don't we do that? You need to replay your life history! Roll film!"

A blur of images shot past. Evinrude got a vague glimpse of fire. Then all was dark again. "The projector's messed up!" Sally exclaimed in dismay.

"I'm so sorry," Evinrude said. "Can I go now?"

"But… but you've got to learn something. It's not right if you don't learn something, and I meant for you to, but then the projector broke, and…"

Evinrude sighed. "Fine. Is there a way you can repair the, ah, projector?"

"Maybe if I asked Raphael? He's an archangel, subs for Peter sometimes, so he knows a bit about tech…"

"Maybe you should."

"Great!" Sally said. "Back in a flash!" She disappeared, leaving Evinrude to waft in the void again. After some time the images appeared again, much slower now and easier to make out. Evinrude saw his life play out before him. He saw again his letters with Eulalie, his encounter with the messenger bird, and his frantic trip to the island where she had died. Once again he saw himself alone in the castle before her ashes, which her grief-stricken parents had collected and preserved in honor in a golden box, and he saw himself secretly pocketing a few of those ashes in a small vial.

The problem was that Sally, in an effort to be as helpful as possible, hadn't just included the parts that he knew. She had included everything relevant to Evinrude's life, whether he had known about it or not.

Evinrude saw Philip of House Shirley make the arrangement to have Eulalie flamed by a dragon. He saw Philip murder Amaryllis and use her death as pretext for a war. He saw himself asking Rowena for help, and Rowena sending him to his death to cover up the truth about her father. He saw Philip becoming king of Loventry, and Rowena becoming Prime Minister. Then, when he had seen everything, Evinrude knew exactly what he wanted.

When the replay was done, Sally reappeared. "Okay!" she said, producing her flashcards again. "It's time to talk about what we learned today! So, who are you, and-"

"I am Evinrude, rightful king of Loventry. And I want it back."

Sally blinked. "Well, you can't! You're dead now, right? You can't just go back and undo things! That's not how this works!"

"Oh, really?" Evinrude said, very calmly. "Then how does it work? As I see it, I was done a grave injustice. I want to remedy it. How do I make that happen?"

"Well…" Sally said helplessly. "Ah. Let me check."

She disappeared into the void. Evinrude wafted about for a moment. Then another voice spoke. "You know, there is another way."

"Who're you?" Evinrude said, alarmed. He looked around for another source of light, but didn't see one. Instead, amidst the shadowy void, he saw one shadow that moved. The shadow spoke, its voice cool.

"Well, I'm not an angel. You might say I belong to the other side. Call me Leon."

"Leon," Evinrude said. He should have said "Begone, foul spirit," or something like it, but against his better judgment he was intrigued. For one thing, he had never before heard of someone from the other side being called Leon. He had assumed their names would sound a lot more sinister.

"Yeah," Leon said, shrugging. "Look, I only have a few moments before the halo-head gets back. So here's my bargain. You want vengeance. You want all kinds of unholy retribution upon all those people what wronged you, right? You know good and well Sally and her crowd aren't going to get it for you. They go in for *forgiveness* and *mercy* and things like that. You want your kingdom back? You want vengeance? You want me."

Evinrude hesitated. "At what price?"

Leon didn't kid around. "Same as it always is."

"When?"

"I'll let you know."

Evinrude nodded slowly. He was dead already, after all. What more did he have to lose if things went wrong? "Fine. It's a bargain."

Leon smiled. "Cool."

There was a flash and a bang of smoke, and they were gone.

Sally reappeared, seconds too late. "Okay, I talked to St. Peter, and we might be able to work something out..." Her voice trailed away uncertainly.   "Evinrude?   Where'd   you   go?"

3: Death on Kirtle Island

The White Beetle Inn on Kirtle Island had experienced a boom in its business of late. The proprietor was not shy in boasting that the Prime Minister of Loventry had used his establishment to conduct her affairs, back before she had assumed her office. Rowena's chair and table had been specially set aside and marked with neat little placards. The proprietor was even considering naming a drink after her.

On this particular summer night, however, one customer did not seem pleased with the sudden fame of the establishment. He sat in another corner of the dining room and glared over at the inoffensive placards. "Rowena," he growled into his mug. "Bah. S'not what I named her, s'not what her mother named her, but does she care? No. Bah."

The general noise of conversation and song in the place was loud enough that no one overheard his grumbling. He considered raising his voice and making a point of it, but changed his mind when he noticed a few Loventry guards over by the front door, their swords plainly visible. Kirtle Island wasn't officially part of the kingdom, but Loventry had been awfully assertive over the past year or so, and the customer decided not to press his luck. With another sullen growl and a spit into his mug, the customer rose from his seat and walked outside. He hadn't left a tip for the barmaid, but he never did anyway. They were only barmaids and he didn't care. He was sure his life was far worse than theirs anyway. Hadn't he fled clear across the ocean and back, wandering from village to village, just to get away from a member of his own magical order?

He shuffled out into the summer night, taking a moment to look up and down the road. A few other passers-by still lingered within view, making it unsafe for him to pull on the battered cloak of disguise he still carried. With a sigh, he turned and headed for the coastline, where he kept a little boat. It had been nice revisiting his old watering hole on Kirtle Island, but he knew he would have to move on.

He had just come within sight of the dock where his boat was moored when a streak of flame split the dark, so bright that he was momentarily blinded. When he recovered his vision, he saw his boat reduced to a burning hulk. Above it, a massive scaly form hovered, its mighty wings tearing at the air. "Any last words?" the dragon rumbled.

"You can't do this!" he protested. "I'm alone! There's no knights about anywhere! There are rules!"

"Yes, you're right," the dragon said, "Normally we wouldn't attack a defenseless person, but you're not exactly defenseless, are you? I've been informed that you're a powerful wizard. Maximilian, Order of the Squirrel."

Now, some wizards might have prudently chosen that moment to deny up and down that they had anything to do with magic whatsoever. This particular wizard, however, had a sore point. Years and years ago, when he was in wizardry school, he had been up for top marks in his class. Unfortunately, he had been beaten out for it by the very same Maximilian whom the dragon appeared to believe he was. Even worse, the class in which Maximilian had edged him out had been a course on Dragon Studies.

Mortimer had held this grudge ever since. Now, here he was mistaken for his arch-rival by a dragon of all things. This sent him into a towering fury. Mortimer whipped out his wand and drew himself up in all his offended dignity. "I ain't Maximilian!" he shouted, "I am Mortimer, Order of the Polecat, father of Rowena, Prime Minister of Loventry!" As emphasis, he conjured a red plasma bolt and sent it streaking into the sky, where it exploded into gaudy fireworks.

The dragon was not particularly impressed. Instead, to Mortimer's surprise, it turned its head a little to the left, towards a nearby dock. "There," it said. "That's what you wanted, isn't it?"

"Yes," said a cool voice from the shadows. Evinrude knew all about Mortimer's grudge, thanks to Leon's helpful insights into the wizard's twisted psyche. Leon had also called up the dragon for him from regions he hadn't been specific about. Now the former crown prince turned and said a quiet word to the dark figure standing next to him, who raised his bow and let fly with a single arrow.

The dragon reeled back in a howl of pain. Mortimer winced. He had never taken an arrow directly to the eye, but he both admired the skill of the shot and hated to imagine how much it had to hurt. He had no particular sympathy for dragons, but didn't wish to draw undue attention to himself, and the dragon really was howling awfully loudly. Quickly he conjured a standard-issue death curse and hit the dragon hard. It collapsed into the harbor, showering him and the other boats with water.

Mortimer ran towards the dock from which the voice had come, already working up another death curse. When he got there, however, he found no one. Soon, all was confusion as the patrons of the White Beetle spilled out into the streets, curious to see what the trouble was, and mightily surprised to find a dead dragon in their island harbor. Mortimer seized the first opportune moment, donned his cloak of disguise, and ran off into the interior of the island, shaking with fear.

He kept going for several hours, climbing into the rugged hills that rose above the White Beetle tavern and the other cluster of buildings that formed the small harbor of Kirtle Island. At last, as the moon rose above him, Mortimer paused in his flight and took a breather. He heard no footsteps behind him, but just to be sure, he set about the usual magical precautions. Mortimer had become quite practiced at these over the past two years. Soon the forest around him was fairly brimming with intruder-alert charms just waiting to sound the alarm about any unsuspecting pursuer. Only when he had set the last charm did Mortimer let himself relax. He slid back against a welcoming tree and sighed. He had hoped to spend the night on board his cabin in the boat, but that was ash and smoldering timbers now. Mortimer swore violently. "Rowena," he exclaimed. "Bah!"

The wizard now had to contemplate his next move. What he wanted more than anything right then was to go to sleep, but first, he supposed, he ought to decide what to do. He no longer had a non-magical way off the island. He could attempt the magical form of transport, but that could be tricky. A proper wizard, somewhat like his daughter, might be able to track him that way if they were able to get hold of one of his socks, and he couldn't say for sure he hadn't left one somewhere. He couldn't stay on the island for long either; all his supplies had gone up in flames with the boat. All he had besides his wand was the small stash of coins in a pouch on his belt, and those weren't as plentiful as he might have wished for.

In the end, Mortimer decided that he could leave the decision until morning. He laid down on the ground, conjured up a rough blanket, and tried to get to sleep. In the morning, he resolved, he'd work out what to do.

Unfortunately, he wouldn't have that luxury. Kirtle Island's police force wasn't terribly vigorous, but it did exist, and it took a dim view of people murdering dragons who were, by all accounts, merely going about their honest business. An examination quickly determined that the arrow wound hadn't been sufficient to kill the dragon, and then one knowledgeable officer found a telltale mark left by Mortimer's death spell. There weren't all that many wizards on Kirtle Island to begin with, and the proprietor of the White Beetle knew a lot more about his customers than it appeared, particularly those that had a habit of stiffing the barmaids. Before too long the officers had sent teams of searchers into the hills to look for Mortimer. They were bound to find him in such numbers, and of course they inevitably did.

Mortimer had overlooked a problem with his carefully laid network of magical charms. He had left no potential approach unguarded, and when one of the Kirtle Island searchers, stumbling in the dark, ran into his intruder-alert charm, it did its job well and let off an ear-splitting shriek of warning. The problem was that Mortimer hadn't thought through what would happen after the alarms went off.

The wizard jolted awake out of an uneasy sleep, and the first thing he saw was several shadowed figures running towards him in the trees. He didn't know that they were only Kirtle Island police watchmen, who had no lethal intent and were only armed with mildly stout sticks. Mortimer, in his half-awake panic, thought they were Polecat wizards coming to take him out, the kind that haunted his nightmares. He responded by unleashing a storm of red lightning bolts in every direction he could.

The trees, and a good many of the unfortunate Kirtle Islanders, promptly went up in flames. Mortimer suddenly realized that the fires were awfully close to him, and that he had very nearly incinerated himself. He bolted in the other direction and promptly set off his own charms. More warning shrieks split the night air, adding to the screams of the injured islanders. Chaos reigned in the woods. Mortimer lost his head entirely, and decided at that moment that the best thing to do was to transport himself away from there as fast as he could. He grabbed in his robe for his spare sock, said the appropriate incantation, and vanished, leaving the wretched Kirtle police to stumble around amidst the burning trees looking for a wizard who was no longer there.

In his haste, however, Mortimer had overlooked the most important rule of magical transportation: always keep one's destination firmly in mind. Without that, one never knows where one might be transported to. In this instance, Mortimer had no destination in mind whatsoever. As a result, his transport spell, lacking any idea where to send him, whisked him to a place that had been on Mortimer's mind recently, or more accurately, on his stomach. The wizard, a little singed, materialized outside the White Beetle. He quickly realized what had happened. Mortimer thought of running, but then decided that what he really needed at that moment was a good stout drink.

Cautiously the wizard approached the door of the White Beetle and found it locked. He knew from past experience that the proprietor slept on premises within the sound of the door and could be stirred out of bed if one knocked hard enough. However, Mortimer decided not to chance it. Instead, he drew his wand and said a quick spell over the doorknob. The lock twisted, and he slipped inside.

All was quiet, the proprietor and everyone else having either gone to bed or gone off in the search for Mortimer. The wizard crept to the bar and conjured up another spell. Soon he was back in his usual seat, a full mug in his hand, staring out the window into the night. "What in blazes do I do now?" he mumbled.

"You could start by answering a few questions," a quiet voice said from behind him. Mortimer started to turn, but something cold and metallic caught him in the back. "I wouldn't move for your wand," the voice said. "I'd run you through before you got anywhere close."

Mortimer suddenly recognized the voice. "You're the one from the docks!" he said.

"Correct," said the voice. "If I'd known you were such an idiot, I wouldn't have my archer friend waste a perfectly good dragon trying to get you captured by the Kirtle Island police. Anyway, you're here now."

"You know my daughter's the Prime Minister of Loventry," Mortimer said, plucking up his courage. "If you harm me, she'll come after you!"

"I doubt it. When was the last time you had contact with her?"

"Recently!" Mortimer said, trying to sound confident. In truth, he hadn't spoken to Rowena since the day she had given him the cloak of disguise, and he didn't particularly want to. It was her fault he was in all these troubles. "And I've taken precautions! She knows I'm here, and I have a messenger raven on standby! It knows to fly off and warn her if I don't come back safe!"

"I see," the voice said. "So, to be clear, if I harm you, the raven tells Rowena and she'll come here and avenge your injury, is that it?"

"Exactly!" Mortimer said, and sighed in great relief. At last he felt things were finally beginning to turn in his favor. It would be the last thought that went through his mind before a solid blow struck his head, knocking him clean unconscious.

When he woke up, he was in the woods again. As his eyes grew accustomed to the light, he realized that he was in a small cave, sitting against one wall. Early morning sunlight filtered in through the cave entrance. Mortimer also realized that he was tied up and that his wand was missing. "Oh, blast," he growled. "What now?"

"You lied about the messenger raven." It was the same voice. Mortimer was beginning to get tired of it. He turned, trying to see who was speaking, but the voice was coming from further inside the cave, lost in its shadows.

"I've been keeping an eye out," the voice continued. "The only ravens that have left this island in the last few hours were official police ravens, likely seeking reinforcements or making reports about the trouble you caused earlier. Also it didn't really make sense anyway; you don't have a room on the island, all you had was your boat, and that was destroyed by the dragon. If you had a raven, where would you have kept it?"

Mortimer spluttered, trying to think of a decent explanation. "I, ah, might have-"

"Don't bother," the voice said. "The point is, you lied. What I want is for Rowena, your daughter, to come to this island. The easiest way for that to happen would have been for you to have been captured by the police after killing the dragon. Alternatively, you could've been injured and your messenger raven could've alerted Rowena, as you explained. But now we can't do that; even if I knock you out again, I can't hire a raven and send it to Rowena, as it'll draw too much attention. So there's only one thing to do."

Mortimer gulped. "Now, wait a minute-"

"Wizards have familial connections through magic, correct? They sense when a family member dies?" There was a flash of steel in the cave.

The Great Hall of Shirleyhold was a truly impressive place, full of mighty stone columns and draped with flowing banners. Rowena detested it, particularly for state business. She preferred to conduct ministerial affairs in her office, a quiet room towards the back of the castle, with high windows that looked out on the courtyard. She had papers arranged neatly on shelves, and a crisp desk intricately carved with runes that were meant to look wizardly and mysterious. In truth, they meant nothing whatsoever; Rowena didn't rely upon runes at all in her magic. She gathered that certain northern wizards did, but she had never gone in for that sort of thing.

The Prime Minister of Loventry sat behind her desk now, paying close attention as the two ambassadors before her each made their case for why King Philip should pick their country as the beneficiary of a particular trade agreement. Neither of them knew that what Philip was really preparing was an invasion, and that the diplomatic efforts were really a way for Rowena to help determine which country was a better and richer target. In the end, it didn't matter overmuch as Philip meant to add both of them to his growing empire. It was all a matter of timing, really.

Rowena studied the two ambassadors as they rattled off various economic statistics and argued about trade forecasts and variable winds. The chief problem in her mind was that Philip's forces were mostly concentrated on land; he hadn't done much with a navy yet. He had griffins and dragons, yes, but the island kingdom which had sent the ambassador on her right, Seyna, was known for its skilled archers. On the other hand, if he struck fast, with the element of surprise, before they had time to get their archers to their posts, then perhaps an attack might work.

The other kingdom, Ilariana, had approachable land routes but was in the south and ringed about by deserts, with the occasional canyon for a change of scenery. It also had extremely high walls, and was built around the only known oasis for miles, which meant it had ready access to water. If Philip attacked there, he would face the distinct possibility of a long siege. Suppose supplies ran short? Dragons and griffins required a great deal of feeding and watering, to say nothing of the army. It presented a real dilemma.

She set the logistical problems aside and brought her mind back to the immediate discussion at hand. The Seynan ambassador, for reasons which escaped her at the moment, was arguing with the Ilarianan about taxation policies. Since Philip meant to conquer both kingdoms eventually anyway and impose whatever taxation he liked, this interested Rowena not at all. Also, she felt she was losing control of the conversation. "Gentlemen," she said, "Perhaps we should resume this in the morning, after you've had a chance to consider. I have set before you King Philip's proposals, which I feel are more than fair-"

Rowena froze. A sudden stinging pain shot through her head, so intense that she almost blacked out. She reeled in her chair, and her aide, a capable woman named Marigold, rushed to her side. "Madam Prime Minister, are you ill?" Marigold said. Both ambassadors had leapt to their feet in alarm, offering hasty assistance.

"No," Rowena said, waving them away, "No, I am not ill. But I am afraid I will need to insist we resume in the morning." She dismissed the ambassadors and her aide without another word, and withdrew as politely and swiftly as she could. Then, safely alone in her quarters, she drew her wand.

Rowena knew what the pain had to mean, of course, but she had to make certain. With a shaking hand, she said the proper incantation. It was one she never would've tried unless she was absolutely desperate. Had it worked, her father would've appeared, greatly aggravated and probably very dirty, in front of her on the floor.

There was a sputter of smoke and a flicker of dust. Nothing else appeared. Rowena's breath caught in her throat. The signs were unmistakable. She knelt down and stared at the small flecks of dust that scattered across the floorboards of her room. Her father was dead. The incantation would have worked otherwise.

The next question, naturally, was what had happened. This required another bit of magic. Rowena took a breath to steady herself. Her emotions were surprisingly mixed after all this time. Part of her, a distant part she hadn't considered for some while, wanted to crawl into a corner and break down over her loss. Another part felt a sense of relief that he was gone, since she didn't have to worry that he might slip up and that her connection to him might be found out. The last chance that her secret would be discovered was finally, hopefully, gone for good.

Carefully she said the words over the flecks of dust. All depended on what happened next. If her father had died of purely natural causes, such as the plague or falling into a river, the dust would turn golden and melt away. She could then say her farewells and put him out of her mind forever. Rowena waited.

The dust did not turn to gold. Instead it flared into bright red sparks that danced angrily on the floorboards and then snapped into black smoke. Rowena swore. That meant her father had been murdered. It was deliberate too; that was the black smoke. Someone, as yet unknown, had sought out her father and cut him down.

She said a final spell, and reached out with her wand, trying to trace the magic back. Perhaps the Polecat assassin, whoever that had been, had finally caught up to Mortimer. But all she could see in her mind was the twisting traces of black smoke, and a faint echo of the tavern where she had last seen her father. Rowena swore again. She had come to the limits of what her magic could do; now she'd have to work the hard way.

Rowena reached for a nearby bell and rang. Marigold dutifully appeared. "Cancel my appointments for tomorrow, and send King Philip my regrets. I have an unexpected journey to make."

4: An Angel Went Down to Loventry

Sally was distraught. From her position in Heaven she had watched events unfold in Loventry below, feeling powerless to help. She believed it was all her responsibility somehow. "I should've gotten him inside the gates sooner!" she wailed. "The other side couldn't have gotten in then!"

Still, despite all her angelic friends' assurances, the damage was done. The other side had indeed gotten to Evinrude, and now he was back on Earth committing murder and who knew what else. Sally felt she had to do something. If the other side could send someone back, why couldn't she?

She had been temporarily relieved of her post as angel on duty at the Pearly Gates; St. Peter was back on watch again. Sally had been reassigned to the Angel Choir; they were always looking for good singers. She should've gone straight over there, she knew. But Sally just couldn't let it go. She had to make things right somehow. So, instead, Sally made her way across the clouds over to the Records Department, housed in a massive marble building flanked in towering columns. She politely tapped on the great doors.

"Excuse me," she said to the angel who answered her inquiring knock. "I'm looking for information on a human? Loventry, not Earth," she added hastily. "I've talked to Constance, not a lot, we're not close personal friends or anything, but she's told me there's other planets with humans on them, and anyway, well, Loventry, please."

"Name?" the angel said.

"Eulalie," Sally replied. "Lady Eulalie of House Turtledove."

"One moment," the angel said.

The concept of a moment's wait is complicated in Heaven, where there are no moments and eternity stretches before you. Sally waited. She whistled a bit. Then she wondered if anyone whistled in the

Angel Choir. Before she could decide, the Records angel returned. "She is," the angel said dramatically, "deceased."

Sally gathered her patience. "I know that," she said, with as much calm as she could manage. "What I would like to know is where she is now. Did she make it here?"

"Ah," the Records angel said. "That will require another search." The angel disappeared. Sally settled in for another wait.

After a long while, the Records angel returned again, looking a little hesitant. "Ah," the angel said. "Well. We have the location of your Lady Eulalie."

"Excellent," Sally said, breathing a sigh of relief. "She's here! Great!"

"No," the Records angel said. "Not exactly."

There was a tremulous pause. "She's not ... in the Bad Place?"

"Oh, no," the Records angel hastened to assure her. "It's not like that. She will make it here, eventually."

Sally blinked. "But... if she's not in Heaven, and she's not, um, down there, where else-" Then she flashed back to her briefing as a stand-in for St. Peter, and realized. "Oh."

"Yes," the Records angel said grimly. "I'm afraid she's in Purgatory."

"Do you know why?" Sally asked. This was important. Purgatory, as all the angels knew, was a mountain with seven levels, corresponding to which non-mortal sin a person had committed. What Eulalie had done to land herself in Purgatory would determine where on the mountain she had landed. Sally was half afraid that this would require a third search through the records and yet another lengthy waiting period.

Happily, the Records angel had anticipated her question. "Oh yes," the angel said. "We double-checked to be certain. She's in Level Three. Wrath, specifically. She didn't go to, well, you know, because she was baptized and went to confession regularly, no mortal sins, so no problem there. But, ah, when she was deceased, it seems she had accumulated a bit of venial sin. Specifically, she was using a great deal of bad language."

Sally blinked again. "And you can go to Purgatory for that?"

"You can," the Records angel said. "She was remarkably inventive. We have the recording, but it is sealed. Only angels with special classifications can unlock it."

"Oh," Sally said, cringing. That meant it was serious. She took a breath and asked the most important question. "How long is she in for?"

"Well…" the angel said. "One's time in Purgatory is not fixed. It depends on how long it takes to purify one's soul of the imperfections of sin. The soul in question might have friends back in the realms of the living offering prayers for her, and so on. So, as to your question, er, it's indeterminate."

"I see," Sally said carefully. "Well, thank you for your time."

"Not at all," the Records angel said, before bowing and closing the great doors. Sally was left alone outside the towering columns of the Records Department to consider what to do. The Records angel had said prayers could spring a soul out of Purgatory, but Sally didn't know if anyone down there was praying for Eulalie. She could dive into Purgatory herself and try to break Lady Eulalie out, of course; that's what an angel like Constance would've done. But then Sally changed her mind. She was, at heart, a less adventurous angel than others, and she didn't want to make trouble. Besides, she was already in enough trouble as it was.

"So…" Constance said, strolling up beside her, "You're just going to leave her down there?"

"Constance!" Sally said with a jump. "Where'd you come from?"

"Oh, I've been around," she said. "That's not important. The thing is, you got Sally in Purgatory; you need to get her out."

"I don't see what I can do!" Sally protested.

"Duh. Go down to Loventry yourself and work the problem. If people aren't praying for Eulalie's soul, get them to! You're an angel! That's what we do!"

"But-"

Constance rolled her eyes. "Honestly. I have to do everything myself around here." She grabbed Sally's arm and pushed her towards the Pearly Gates. She didn't pause to think about how to explain their mission to St. Peter, but fortunately, she wouldn't have to. She would learn later that another world had exploded, which had resulted in quite a lot of its people having to be processed on an emergency basis into Heaven. In the meantime, in the short gap between his absence and a substitute angel taking his place as gatekeeper, Constance charged though, dragging Sally with her.

"But-" Sally said.

"Have fun!" Constance said. "Do what I would do! Or maybe what I wouldn't do. Whatever you do, don't destroy the world. Long story. Anyway. Save souls! Be angelic!" She gave Sally a final shove into the clouds. Then, satisfied, she raised her own wings and vanished. She had her own business back on Earth, after all.

As with magical transportation, it is likewise important when flying down from Heaven to keep one's destination firmly in mind. With so many mortal worlds out there these days, one could intend to land on Earth and instead find oneself on the planet ruled by intelligent salamanders. One does not want to land on Salamander World. Fortunately, though caught off guard, Sally had just enough presence of mind in the descent to catch herself, spread her wings, and fix Loventry in her mind. She flashed through clouds and past colorful pictures of other worlds she had never seen until, with a bump and a jolt, she landed in Loventry.

Carefully, Sally got to her feet, gathered herself, and looked around. She had landed in a forest, and she could see castle towers looming distantly over the trees. She could also hear the roar of the ocean faintly in the distance. That meant she was probably where she wanted to be, smack on Isle Turtledove, home of the late Lady Eulalie. Sally straightened her halo, checked that her sword was in position, made sure her invisibility was on, and started towards the castle.

She formed a basic plan as she made her way there. She would hang around a bit invisibly, observe, and determine who Eulalie's friends were. Then she would assume a visible human form, reveal herself, and organize the prayer group. This seemed the easiest way to go about it. With her plan settled, Sally found herself quite enjoying her walk through the human world. The evening sun glowed calmly through the trees, and colorful birds dashed here and there across the branches, leaves fluttering in their wake. She rounded a corner at last and found herself facing a long stretch of golden sand, sloping down towards the tall grey towers of Turtledove Castle.

Sally gasped. She wasn't alone. The sand was filled with marching soldiers, an entire squadron of knights in armor, all busily charging about and drilling for battle. Sally hadn't expected to walk into preparations for a battle, especially when she had no idea whom they were planning to fight. The one thing she knew for certain was that she wanted no part of it. This looked to be a human fight and was probably nothing to do with her mission to save Lady Eulalie.

Sally made her way gingerly around the edge of the sand, dodging the marching knights as she went. She could see the castle walls beyond with a pair of stolid gates right in the center, and she aimed for that. Sally hoped she could slip inside and search out Eulalie's friends without being detected. Being invisible, she assumed this wouldn't be too difficult.

She had almost reached the gates when one of the knights, a captain presumably, abruptly clambered up on a rise and bawled out, "All right, you lot! Everyone inside! Mess line forms on the right!" With that, the knights surged in a pack straight towards the gates. Sally was right in their path.

She panicked, as anyone would do when faced with a charging force of armed and hungry men coming straight at them. Sally was, moreover, not a combat angel and was unused to dealing with recalcitrant mortals. Her prior excursions to the mortal world had mostly involved Search and Rescue missions: saving people from natural disasters, getting lost, and similar mishaps. She hadn't been trained for this. As a result Sally did the first thing that sprang to mind: she reached out and tried to supernaturally move the knights out of the way. Unfortunately it had been a while since she had tried this particular miracle, and she misjudged her own strength.

A wave of light crackled across the sand. The knights tumbled backwards in a clanging of armor, shouting in alarm as they fell. Sally panicked, whirled, and ran through the gates, finding herself in a grassy courtyard. Servants and more knights were running towards her, drawn by the shouting beyond the walls. It occurred to Sally then, even in her panic, that she hadn't realized House Turtledove had quite this many soldiers sworn to its banner. She wondered if perhaps she should have reviewed the records on the island before she made the journey.

She dodged rapidly through the crowd, bent on finding a place to hide and wait until everything calmed down and she could resume her mission. The castle loomed above her, and she noticed a large pair of oak doors open directly ahead. Sally, more out of desperation than angelic intuition, ran towards it.

Inside she soon found herself wandering through a veritable warren of gloomy castle corridors, lit with guttering candles and adorned with tapestries of somber-faced people. Sally couldn't help but think what kind of a childhood Eulalie must have had, growing up in such a depressing place. After about an hour, she also couldn't help but notice that she was completely lost. Not only did she have no idea where the chapel was, she didn't even know where she herself was, nor how to get out again.

Sally was on the point of reaching for her halo to buzz Heaven and ask for a location check when she rounded a corner and nearly collided with a furtive man in a cloak hurrying down the hall. "Oh, I'm sorry!" Sally apologized.

"Who's there?" the man yelped, jerking away and looking wildly around.

Sally decided there was nothing else for it. On her previous Search and Rescue trips to the mortal world she had been trained never to reveal herself to the humans unless absolutely necessary. On the other hand, she'd practically done it already, and besides she needed help badly. She lowered her invisibility and powered up her angelic glow. "Hello there," she said, trying to project a calming presence. "Look, don't be alarmed. I'm not going to hurt you. I'm an angel!"

"Ah," the man said, laughing a little. "So you're the cause of all that commotion out on the parade ground earlier. I was wondering about that. Amusing as it was to watch, I didn't think they'd all tripped over themselves entirely on their own."

"Sorry," Sally apologized again. "It was an accident. I was trying to get in here to find the chapel, and, well…"

"What luck," the man said, "I'm actually going there myself. I'm Father Thomas, you see. I'm the castle chaplain. Or I was. It's rather complicated just now."

"Oh," Sally said. Then she had a sudden burst of hope. "You're not on your way to a Mass, are you?"

"No," he said sadly. "We're only able to do that once a week now, at night if we're careful. I've only come today for confessions, and I can't stay long. We're in a bit of trouble, you see."

"What kind of trouble?" Sally said, her curiosity piqued.

"Well, you see, ever since Lady Eulalie died-" There was a slight catch in his voice. "I expect you'll know about that. You being an angel and all."

"Oh, yes," Sally said. "I actually wanted to ask about that. You wouldn't know her, would you?"

"Know her?" Father Thomas said. Even in the shadows of the corridor, Sally could see the look of anguish on his face. "I baptized her. I watched her grow up. She was there every Sunday with her parents, and then…"

"And then the dragon," Sally said sympathetically.

"Yes," Father Thomas said. "We were all devastated. We've never had troubles with dragons before. And then suddenly Philip became king and there was the war, and he stationed soldiers here for our security, he said, and somehow… well, his men haven't left. What remains of House Turtledove is under lock and key. No one is allowed on or off the island except by permission. The castle itself is under guard as well, and the chapel has been officially closed."

Sally's eyes were wide. "But how can you-"

"We go on," Father Thomas said, with a shrug. "There were two fathers here, but Father Raymond was locked up, so now there's just me. I hold service in secret. People come in as they can. I hear confession as I can. One manages."

The angel's hand tightened round the hilt of her sword. "It's not right."

"Well, no, I won't disagree with you there," Father Thomas said, with a sad little laugh. "And as I said, I did enjoy seeing the knights falling all over themselves around the courtyard. But unless you're playing on staying around and doing that to the king's entire army, there's not much that can be done. And, I am sorry, but I do need to hurry along. As I said before, I can only stay-"

"Oh, right, yes," Sally said, "The chapel, yes. Can I come?"

"Of course," Father Thomas said. "But on one condition." He beckoned her to follow him as he started swiftly down the corridor. "As you are an angel, tell me, how is Eulalie? Is she… up there?"

Sally didn't know what to say. As an angel, she couldn't lie. The very thought of it went against her angelic nature. Even a fourth-class angel such as she knew that the smallest of lies could start one on a path that eventually led to the Infernal Regions. Sally had no intention of going there at all. On the other hand, she could see how much Father Thomas cared for Lady Eulalie. Could she tell him now that Eulalie hadn't made it into Heaven, and that in fact she was condemned for who knew how long in the burning fires of Purgatory? On the bright side, she considered, he could help get her out, so there was that.

"Well, ah-" Sally began.

All at once their conversation was interrupted by an angry shout. "You there! Who are you! Show yourselves!"

They both turned. At the other end of the corridor two guards in dark armor stood with swords drawn, and they did not look particularly welcoming.

"Oh, blast," Father Thomas said. "I mistimed it. They're usually not on patrol through here for an hour yet."

The guards advanced. "You're that chaplain, aren't you?" one of them snarled. "Didn't we arrest you once already?"

"I do seem to recall that, yes," Father Thomas said. "You put me in a boat and told me not to come back to the island, if I remember right."

"And yet here you are."

"Here I am," the chaplain said coolly. "Here I will always be. Where I am needed."

"Now, look," Sally cut in. "I'm not sure what's going on, but maybe we can talk about-"

The first guard had ignored Sally, and was instead sizing up the chaplain. "Yeah. You're going to keep on coming back, aren't you?"

Thomas looked at him straight on. "I am."

"Then there's really only one way to solve this, isn't there?"

"I expect so."

"Wait a minute," Sally said, with growing alarm, "You can't just-"

But they could. Without another word, the guard cut Father Thomas down with one blow of his sword. The chaplain crumpled to the ground, killed instantly. The other guard started towards Sally, intent on inflicting upon her the same fate.

He never had the chance. The angel, shocked beyond measure, reacted out of pure righteous instinctual fury. Light exploded from her hand, blasting the two men through the corridor wall and into the open night air beyond. As more guards came running, Sally turned upon them, blasting them away in turn. Several of the remaining guards tried to flee. Sally grabbed one and slammed him against the remnants of a wall. "Where're you keeping the family?" she screamed, as light blazed around her. "Talk!"

The guard, terrified, told her everything. Sally flung him aside like a child's toy and stormed off. The deliverance of Isle Turtledove had begun.

5: The Paragon Sets Sail

Philip didn't learn until the following morning that Isle Turtledove was in revolt against his benevolent rule. When he received the news in his council room in the castle of Shirleyhold, he had been preoccupied with other pressing matters. He had expected to receive a report from Rowena about which kingdom he should invade next, and he was somewhat annoyed to learn that she had taken off on an undisclosed errand of her own. Philip had also received word that Kirtle Island was all in confusion; evidently someone as yet unknown had killed a dragon there, along with several members of its police force, leaving the whole place in turmoil.

This was not the best time to find out that yet another part of his kingdom had gone and gotten itself in trouble. Philip swore violently at the hapless messenger who had delivered the news. "*What* attacked the guards?" he shouted.

"A lady," the messenger said, shaking. He had heard vague rumors of people who displeased Philip finding themselves getting flamed by the dragons in the army, and he didn't particularly fancy that. "A shining lady. She glowed."

"She glowed," Philip repeated.

"And knocked the walls down. She blasted them. With light. "

"I see," Philip said coldly. "And instead of attacking her, my soldiers heroically ran away, is that it?"

The messenger had no good answer to this, so he wisely said nothing. Philip went on. "And now you don't know where the rest of House Turtledove is, you don't know who's in control of the island, and you don't know where this whatever-she-is might be now, or what she wants. Does that sum up the situation?"

The terrified messenger could only nod.

Philip could have thrown him to the dragons, but he decided that the messenger wasn't worth the bother. Besides, it occurred to him that he needed the man anyway. "I want you to go to the raven quarters and send the fastest bird they have to find the Prime Minister. I want her back here as quickly as possible."

The messenger nodded again, feeling relieved, and began to go. Philip held up a hand, and then withdrew a small scroll from his pocket. "Also, tell them to send another raven to this tavern, to the room of Alistair, and give him this. He's a wizard, never mind what order. He'll know what it's about."

The messenger took the scroll and ran, grateful that he had gotten away. Philip ignored his departure. Even after Rowena had become his Prime Minister, he had made sure to maintain his connections to the Polecat wizards House Shirley had allied itself with over the years, believing they might come in useful down the line. They'd helped him set up Amaryllis, among other things, by intercepting Evinrude's mail and convincing her that Evinrude had been unfaithful with Eulalie. They could help him out again.

Within the hour, two ravens were winging swiftly away from Shirleyhold, headed in different directions. One flew west, towards the distant Kirtle Island where Rowena was headed to find who had murdered her father. The other flew towards a much closer destination, a small roadside inn a few hours away, where two roads met at a crossing in a dense wood.

This inn, unlike its distant counterpart on Kirtle Island, was a lot dingier and dirtier. It had loads of smoke-filled rooms and an accompanying crowd of unsavory people, and the only reason a constable would've gone near the place was if he were in hot pursuit of a lawbreaker. Alistair had become quite comfortable there and had done quite a lot of business in the bargain. He was reclining now in his room, studying up on the latest Polecat wizardry techniques, when the raven fluttered in his window. The raven stared at him, nodded slightly, and squawked his name. "That's me," Alistair said. "What's up?"

The raven dropped the scroll before him and waited. Alistair looked down at the scroll. It was a simple random phrase, completely unintelligible to a random person if it fell into the wrong hands. To

Alistair, of course, it meant that Philip wanted his services in an urgent matter. "I hope it's more important than sifting through mail," he groused. "I mean, really, I'm a respected wizard of the Polecat Order. Intercepting love notes between Evinrude and what's her name, the girl who got flamed? Child's play."

The raven squawked again at him. It evidently didn't care at all about his grievances. Alistair rolled his eyes and, turning back to business, quickly scrawled the code word that meant he accepted Philip's orders. Then he waved the raven away. It darted out the window in an offended flurry of wings, and Alistair began to pack.

Then he heard a knock at his door. "I'm sorry," he said, "I'm not available for new business just now-"

The door banged open. "Yeah, you wouldn't be," Leon said. "Yikes, this place is a dump. Philip doesn't pay you much, does he?"

Alistair stepped back in alarm, preparing to conjure a lightning bolt in defense. "Who're you?" It only then occurred to him to wonder how the man knew he was associated with Philip.

He would never get the chance to ask. "Let's just say I'm working with someone who pays better," Leon said, before unleashing a blast of flame. He enjoyed it so much that he let the fire spread without bothering to hold it back. Leon walked casually away into the morning light as the inn blazed away behind him. He glanced up at the raven winging its way back towards Shirleyhold and considered shooting it down, but then decided against it. It would be more fun to keep Philip guessing anyway.

Rowena, meanwhile, had arrived on Kirtle Island the day before to find it in a state of chaos. The chief of police and his second in command had perished up in the hills, and as a result, no one was left in command of the island. A very large dragon corpse lay smoldering in the island's main harbor, and as this wasn't a problem the islanders usually faced, no one knew what to do with it. They had tried lifting it out with ropes, but dragons, even dead ones, are exceptionally heavy. If there were any wizards left on Kirtle who could've lent magical help, they weren't showing themselves. Given the mood of the islanders towards wizards just then, this seemed to be the smart play.

The Prime Minister of Loventry, however, was no ordinary wizard. As soon as Rowena had set foot on the island and taken stock of the situation, she set to work. She rounded up what remained of the island police and deputized the first capable man she saw to be its leader. "I want order restored," she shouted. "Curfew imposed at once. No one steps outside their doors after nightfall. All swords except those in official hands are to be sheathed or confiscated. A drawn sword means arrest." She motioned to the crowd of onlookers that had gathered around them. "And get everyone back in their homes, *now!*"

"What about the dragon, ma'am?" the newly appointed chief of police asked, a little tremulously.

"I shall deal with the dragon myself," Rowena said in a voice that brooked no dissent. The policemen scattered before her. Within moments she was alone in the harbor, staring at the looming corpse of the dragon. A wave of stench met her; the dragon had been dead for several days. Nonetheless she steadied herself and examined it closely. She soon found the mark left by her father's death spell and recognized it at once. Rowena quickly shook off the small pang of emotion she felt, aware that islanders might be watching her from a distance. She took a breath and pressed on.

Then she found the arrow. In all the confusion, no one among the islanders had gotten around to removing it from the dragon's eye. Rowena smiled grimly. She knew her father was horrible at archery, and she doubted very much that these middling islander folk had the skills to bring down a dragon by arrow-shot. Whoever had done this was almost certainly associated with the one who had slain her father.

Rowena drew her wand. She tapped the arrow gently with it, already sensing an air of crisp professionalism, a sort of deadly courtesy and skill. Something about this unsettled her. She set her feelings aside for the moment and concentrated on the magical link to the archer. She expected that it might lead to some distant country that would require a long journey; any sensible person who had slain a powerful wizard and killed a dragon, and set in motion a plan so obviously intricate as this must have been, would surely have withdrawn to a place of safety many miles away. To her astonishment, the trace was still bright and clear. The archer was close, she realized. She turned in astonishment and even said a confirmatory spell. Her wand flashed in her hand. The assassin was staying at the White Beetle Inn.

She took this as a personal insult. Rowena had spent many years living and doing business at the White Beetle; it was almost like home to her. Knowing that the murderer of her father was staying there felt like the worst of betrayals. Fury boiled up within her and she stormed towards the tavern, wand blazing in her hand. When the police chief approached to report that her orders had been carried out and order had been thoroughly restored, she brushed right past him without so much as an acknowledgement of his existence.

Rowena blasted in the main room and looked around. She saw him at once. The man was lounging at a table only a corner away from her own, kicking back in his chair, obviously well in his cups. Behind him, she saw a bow and a quiver of arrows carelessly thrown on the floor. The magical traces led right to him. Rowena descended upon him in towering wrath. "You," she snarled, "You murdered my father."

The man spluttered. "Who the heck are you?"

"Why?" Rowena demanded.

"I wanna know!" he said, aggrieved. "I don't do murder, I'm an honest mercenary! I do work for what I'm hired! Best archer around anywhere, that's what I am! But I don't do murder!"

Rowena paused. "You're a mercenary."

"I am!" the man said. "And as I said, I don't do murder! I don't do women, or kids, or civilians! I do dragons mostly, also soldiers, robbers, and the occasional burglar, if times are slow."

"I see," Rowena said. This she hadn't foreseen. It also meant a problem. The law of magical linking only went so far. It could lead her to the person who had struck the blow that killed the dragon, but not the person who hired the killer, since there was no magical connection between them. The man and his employer had only exchanged money, that was all, no sorcery or wizardry involved. That meant she would have to resort to old-fashioned methods.

"So," she said, gathering herself, "You wanted to know who I am?"

"Actually," the man said, sensing danger, "I don't really, I can go, honest I can…"

"Sorry," Rowena said, "I am Prime Minister of Loventry. I am also a wizard of the order of the Rabbit. I want to know who killed my father. I don't think you did. But you were hired by the one who may have. So. Who hired you?"

"Look, I'd love to tell you, I really would," the man said, "but as a mercenary, I'm bound by contracts. We take 'em very seriously, we really do, and we don't disclose who hired-"

Rowena drew her wand. "Then we'll have to do this the hard way." In truth she didn't entirely intend on ripping the information from the man's mind just yet. She found that sort of thing distasteful, and besides, she wasn't as skilled as other wizards, particularly the darker ones, at sorceries of that nature. For all she knew she wouldn't end up with the right thoughts and would have a random fragment of a rude drinking song stuck in her brain for the rest of her life. Hopefully, however, the mercenary wouldn't know that.

The man took a breath. "You have to understand," he said, "there are ways these things work. Y' don't just walk into some place and hire someone like me. There's channels. Procedures. I don't even know his name."

"Then how did he hire you?" Rowena said patiently.

"He left a letter with m' courier," the mercenary said. "The courier delivered it to the captain, who assigned it to me. That's how I got it. I don't even know the whole job; I only know what I was told. I had my instructions, and I followed them. I got paid through the captain. All right?"

"Do you still have the letter?" Rowena asked.

"No," the man said. "We destroy everything like that after the job's done. Mercenary policy."

"I don't suppose you destroyed it magically, did you?"

"Oh no," the mercenary said. "We know a bit about you wizard types, you trace things with magic. We did it with fire, then scattered the ashes. Mercenary-"

"Policy," Rowena interrupted. She glanced around; the main room of the tavern was quite empty, except for herself and the mercenary. "I take the point. Where do I find this courier?"

"Not here," the man said. "He's in Ilariana."

"Where?" Rowena said. "What building? Why Ilariana?"

"As to why," the man said, "Because that's where the Mercenary Guild headquarters is. We're organized, y'know, we've got ourselves sorted. Now, where I can't tell you. It's a secret, you know, kept hidden, so you types can't-"

"Shut up," Rowena said and struck him with a death curse she had begun conjuring from the moment he had given her the courier's location. The Prime Minister had already decided to kill him once the conversation was over, and she was certain they were alone.

She had never directly murdered a human before, even in the days when she had fled her old home to escape her family and her old identity. She had arranged for killings, sure, passed along information or given orders, but she had never actually struck the blow before. Rowena had clung to that last remnant of her identity as a member of the Rabbit order.

Now, however, she knew she couldn't let this man go. He knew her identity and her intentions. She couldn't take him with her as a prisoner; he would be a liability on the way and might escape. The same problem applied if she handed him off as a prisoner to the local police force. Moreover, if she did that, they might ask why she wanted him held, which meant she would have to explain about her father. Above all, she had to keep that secret.

She stared at the slain mercenary on the floor. She had performed the death curse before, always in battle against dragons or other creatures, but never against a human being. Rowena could feel the magical backwash against her soul, almost as if she had plunged her wand hand into a bath of icy water. She shivered for a moment, knowing that she could never truly be a Rabbit again.

Then Rowena closed her eyes and tried to set her feelings aside as best she could. When she opened her eyes again, her primary thought was what to do with the body. After a moment, she decided that the innkeeper could deal with it.

With that question settled, Rowena left the White Beetle inn without looking back. She reached into her pocket, but felt nothing. Rowena swore violently. She always carried a spare sock with her, but she must have forgotten it in her haste. Without it, she couldn't engage in the usual pathways of magical transport. She was going to have to go the hard way.

She saw the police chief arguing with some affronted islanders who didn't take kindly to having their swords confiscated. Rowena cut into the dispute, ignoring the outraged islanders. "I require transport to Ilariana," she said. "I'll need the fastest ship available. See to it, and have it prepared within the hour."

"Yes, ma'am," the chief said. He saluted, and then hurried off, glad to have something to do that didn't require being in the immediate area. Rowena turned to the islanders, and her wand flashed in her hand.

"Back to your homes," she said. "*Now.*"

They scattered before her. Rowena, for the first time that day, almost smiled.

The police chief, new as he was to his post, did know something about ships. He quickly found the fastest ship in Kirtle Island, one which happily had not suffered damage when a large dragon corpse had splashed down into the harbor as several other ships had done. He commandeered the ship and pressed into service several officers and unhappy islanders to fill out its crew, then presented Rowena with it when she arrived at the docks. "It'll do," she said, climbing on board.

The captain of the ship, somewhat aggrieved at being diverted from his intended course, asked grumpily when she wanted to set sail for Ilariana. "Now," she said. "Where's your cabin?"

He pointed it out.

"Fine," Rowena said. "I'll be in there. I do not expect to be disturbed."

The door of the captain's cabin summarily slammed behind her. The captain hadn't even had a chance to retrieve his belongings. He was more than somewhat aggrieved now, but it couldn't be helped. One didn't interfere with the Prime Minister of King Philip, no matter how much one didn't like her.

And so the ship, the *Paragon* by name, set sail on a course southwards. The wind was with them and filled out the sails nicely. Rowena did not emerge from the cabin, and the crew gave her a wide berth. The captain would, under normal circumstances, have sent someone to inquire if she needed any food or drink or anything, as he would do for a special guest to whom he had lent his cabin. But as he had not lent it but rather had it appropriated out from under him, the captain didn't feel any particular need to be hospitable. Besides, he reasoned, she was a wizard; she had her wand, hadn't she? She could very well magic up some provisions herself.

Rowena, staring out of the window into the sunset, wasn't in a mood to magic up anything in the way of provisions. She stayed there, staring out the window, all through the night.

It was in the morning that Philip's raven found the *Paragon*. The ship had made good time, having caught a fair southerly wind all that night. The captain expected that they would make landfall by the next morning, at the port of a city called Miralycia. From there, as Ilariana was inland, Rowena could expect to find her own transport. The captain would be quite glad to be rid of her.

Then the raven flopped tiredly onto the deck of the *Paragon* and squawked her name. The captain sighed. "She's in my cabin," he said. "One moment." He motioned to his first mate to take the raven to the galley for some scraps and then headed for his cabin.

He hesitated before knocking. Rowena had said, with no hesitation, that she did not want to be disturbed. On the other hand, the captain had also recognized the raven's markings and realized that this was a royal messenger raven, which meant that the message was extremely important. The captain sighed, wishing (not for the last time) that he had never chosen to make Kirtle Island a stop on his regular trading route. Then he screwed up his courage and knocked.

There was a slight, breathless pause. Then the door opened. "What?" Rowena said.

The captain couldn't quite tell if she sounded angry, pleasant, or just tired. He took a chance. "There's a messenger raven for you, ma'am," he said. "Came in just now."

The door creaked open. Rowena stood there, wand in hand. "Well?" she said.

Just then the captain realized his error. "It's, ah, in the galley. The raven is. I sent it with the first mate to get scraps. It's a courtesy, you see-"

"I do see," Rowena said. She was definitely angry. "A messenger raven arrives, sufficient cause for you to disturb me when I requested not to be disturbed, and instead of bringing the message to me directly so I could read it in private, as befits a Prime Minister, you send it off to the galley where any one of your crew could take it from the raven and read it for themselves?"

"Well-" the captain began. "It's a courtesy-"

"And this is a mercy," Rowena said and blasted the captain with a death curse. This time she felt the cold a little less.

She had worked it out already. Rabbit wizards, especially council ones, were sensitive about these things. Once they met her face to face, they would be able to tell what she had done. She had no choice now. She might just as well join up with the Polecats. And if she was going to be a Polecat, well, she'd had an excellent teacher.

She stormed out of the cabin and made her way to the galley. The first mate was there, amiably chatting with the ship's cook as the messenger raven gobbled up table scraps tossed to it by a few kitchen boys. "You," Rowena snapped to the first mate, who immediately came to attention. She had forgotten his name. "You're the captain now. You'd better see to the ship. You'll find your predecessor outside my cabin. The rest of you, out." She moved to the messenger raven. The first mate had already left the kitchen; the kitchen boys and the cook quickly followed. Rowena examined the raven. It eyed her and squawked her name.

She nodded. "That's me. The message?"

The raven lifted its leg. Rowena unbound the small scroll tied to it. To her astonishment, it wasn't even written in Philip's hand. It was a peremptory order in his name, issued under the royal seal, requiring her to return to Shirleyhold immediately. He hadn't even given her the courtesy of an explanation.

Rowena was on the point of writing the foulest expletive she could think of as a reply and sending it back. She would have done, but then again, she wasn't sure yet that she wanted to break with Philip. For one thing, he had contacts with Polecat wizards, and she suspected she might need them, particularly if the Rabbits decided to come after their former member.

Thus, instead of an expletive, Rowena took the scroll and wrote down the usual code word that served as her reply. "Return as swiftly as you can," she told the raven. "I won't be far behind."

The raven fluttered swiftly away from the ship. Not many of the ship's crew noticed its departure, except for one huddled figure near the stern. The figure noted its flight path and waited to see what the ship would do. Sure enough, the *Paragon* slowly came about and headed eastward again, back towards Loventry.

Evinrude scowled. His original plan to draw Rowena away from Philip and into Ilariana chasing after mercenaries so he could confront her in the shadows had gone somewhat askew. Still, he hadn't come back from the other side of death to be thrown off course now. He had sent Leon back to Loventry, working to cut Philip off from the support of his wizards. That was part of the deal they had made. Evinrude stared at the sea as it slowly turned dark, reflecting the night above, while he worked to devise a new plan. The *Paragon* kept sailing eastward, Rowena in command, unaware.

The Ballad of Evinrude and Eulalie

6: Angels Assemble

While the *Paragon* was making its way back home towards Loventry, Sally was rapidly realizing that she had no idea what to do with a rebellion after she had started it. It had all gone so well at first. With angelic power she had driven the soldiers from Isle Turtledove, sending them scattering from its shores in terror. She had then marched through the castle, searching out the prison cells and liberating each and every one of the imprisoned Turtledove loyalists, right down to Lady Eulalie's unfortunate parents. Sally promptly declared that they were restored to power. "That's it then," she said, in rather an anticlimactic way. "Congratulations."

"Thanks," Lady Eulalie's father said. "But-"

Sally had already turned away. "Oh," she said, pausing. "I'm sorry, what?"

"But what happens when the soldiers come back?" Lady Eulalie's father said. "Are you staying?"

Sally hadn't thought that far. "Ah…"

"We've only got a few knights and no weapons at all," Eulalie's father pleaded. "They confiscated everything. If you leave, and they come back in force, we'll be slaughtered for sure."

"And there's the food situation," Eulalie's mother said. "The garrison stripped the castle pantry dry, I'm afraid. We don't have much land allotted to us; it's pretty much the island and the fishing grounds around it. We survive off trade and alliances with other houses, along with what people make and grow here, and the garrison put a crimp in all that for a while. Unless you can help with that, we're going to be starving pretty soon. And winter isn't all that far off."

"Oh dear," Sally said. She hadn't thought about winter either. One didn't think too much about the weather in Heaven, where time itself is immaterial. "Well, you see…"

She considered the problem. Her mission was to get Lady Eulalie out of Purgatory. To do that, she needed prayer. In a sense, now, her mission was accomplished. All she needed to do was to have a quick word with Father Raymond, the castle's new chaplain, to get the process going, and she could be on her way back to the Pearly Gates. Her task was done now, wasn't it?

And yet… "No," she said, "I'm not leaving. I shall stay and assist."

Lady Eulalie's parents were extremely relieved, as was Father Raymond. Sally was hugged and thanked many times over, and Father Raymond asked if there was anything he could do to assist. "Actually, there is," Sally said, and pulled him aside for a quiet word after sending Lady Eulalie's grateful parents away. She then explained, as circumspectly as she could, that she needed prayers said for Eulalie's soul, the sooner the better. The chaplain got the drift. "I'll get that started right away," he said, and hurried off to the chapel.

"Right," Sally said. "Now what?" She didn't know how long it would take to get Lady Eulalie out of Purgatory, and even then she would have to arrange something in order to get her resurrected, undoing Philip's murder by dragon. She also needed to stop Evinrude from his course of vengeance, and figure out how to set the country of Loventry right again. She couldn't do all that and stay with Isle Turtledove to help them in their hour of peril. "What I need," she realized, "is backup!"

There was only one angel she could think of who she could call on for that. Besides, she felt primly, it was only fair; Constance had gotten her into this mess in the first place; she ought to help get her out of it.

Sally withdrew to a quiet corner of the castle, reached for her halo, and tapped it, carefully. It chimed in a soft, welcoming way. "Angelic Communications," said an ethereal voice. "This is Claire, how might I assist you?"

"Hi," Sally said. "I'd like to speak to Constance, please."

"One moment," Claire said. There was the faint sound of harps playing a golden melody. Sally settled in for a wait; she'd grown accustomed to this by now. It was a slightly different experience in the mortal world, of course; here she could actually watch an ant crawl across the castle stones and count the minutes ticking by.

Then, at last, a sharp voice came across her halo. "Yeah?"

"Hello," Sally began tentatively. "I'm Sally, and I was wondering if you might be able to help me. I'm in a little bit of trouble."

"Hang on!" the voice snapped. There was a sudden roar. Sally was taken aback. She hoped she hadn't interrupted something.

"Are you all right?" she inquired.

She heard more roaring, and a crash that sounded like something very large had been thrown into a pile of leaves and dirt. The roar that followed strongly suggested that whatever had been thrown very much disapproved of the experience. "Yeah," the voice said, very strained. "Just fighting a resurrected bear, one sec!"

Sally blinked. "Fighting a what?"

There was no response. She wondered if she had lost the connection. She didn't think she had; the halo network was pretty much perfect, and therefore by definition one, couldn't lose it. Sally sighed, and waited yet again. She was beginning to get used to it.

Meanwhile, at the other end of the connection, Constance, as she had attempted to explain, was fighting a bear. Specifically, it was a very large grizzly bear she had brought to life. She had recently spent some time rolling around with a group of pandas, and she had been misled into thinking that all bears would be cute and cuddly just like the pandas. As a result, when she had resurrected the grizzly bear on her return trip to North America, she had assumed it would be just as cuddly as the pandas.

Unfortunately, she made a critical mistake. The bear she chose to resurrect was a mama bear, and Constance had thoughtfully chosen to resurrect the cubs along with it. The mama grizzly bear, upon returning to life, saw Constance and perceived her as a threat to the cubs. She promptly did what all mama bears do when their cubs are threatened and charged forward in a burst of savage power.

Constance backpedaled as swiftly as she could. At first she tried frantically reasoning with the mama bear. "Look, I mean you no harm, I'm sorry, I'm only trying to help, just *calm down,* okay?" The bear didn't seem to be listening. It kept thundering forward, roaring tremendously and tearing for Constance's head with its mighty paws. Constance kept backpedaling but suddenly ran hard up against a tree. It was at this unfortunate moment that Sally had buzzed in.

Constance had no choice; she grabbed her halo and hurled it at the bear, blasting it backwards in an explosion of golden light. Unfortunately, she hadn't hit it hard enough to knock it out; she hadn't quite unleashed everything she had, not wanting to kill the bear again after having gone to the trouble of resurrecting it. As a result, the mama bear came roaring right back up, immensely more agitated than before. Constance had only one option left. She glanced up, saw a patch of blue sky above her, and took to it, her wings flying. The bear was left bewildered on the ground, not quite used to its prey taking flight just when it was cornered. Constance rocketed into the open air, relieved that she had gotten away. She knew technically she wouldn't have been harmed in any case, being an angel, but she might have dented her halo, and that would've been wildly embarrassing. She'd already gotten in trouble for that with Winifred, her superior in the Heavenly Hosts, after visiting the pandas.

She took a moment, hovering in the air above the forest, to regain her composure, then summoned her halo to her. Constance tapped it lightly. Sally's voice came tentatively. "Yes?"

"Yeah," Constance said. "So, what's going on? You're saving Loventry, resurrecting what's her name, kicking demon butt, right?"

It took Sally a moment to explain everything that was happening. For one thing, Constance hadn't fully paid attention to all the nuances of the story the first time around, so Sally had to explain some bits about Evinrude and Amaryllis all over again. With some angels she might have had to do a long sidebar about the existence of other worlds, but fortunately Constance was already well accustomed to that reality. "Been there, done that," Constance said. "It's why you called, yeah?"

"Yes," Sally said. "So, basically, I need to stop Evinrude on his mission of vengeance, save Lady Eulalie from Purgatory, and restore the kingdom of Loventry. Can you help?"

"What about what's-her-face?" Constance said. "The girl who got shot by the arrow?"

Sally blinked. In all the fuss, she had honestly forgotten about Lady Amaryllis. "Oh, um…"

"Lesson one," Constance said, "Everyone matters. You save one person, you save 'em all."

"Oh," Sally said. "Of course! I knew that, I'm an angel!"

"Right," Constance said dryly. "Also, it'll tidy things up. If we can bring Evinrude back to the good side, maybe he can sort things out, marry the girl, bam, problem all solved. So, first, we know where Eulalie is. Do we know where Amaryllis is? Please don't say the Bad Place. I've been there, and it's not fun."

Sally shivered piously. She couldn't imagine what it must have been like for an angel, good and true, to descend into the Infernal Regions. "I don't know, but I can check with Records," she offered. "It might take a while, of course. They're a bit slow."

Constance smiled. "Hang on. These things have conferencing now, right?" She tapped her halo in a particular place. "Hey. It's me. Loop in Monica, will you?" There was a short pause. "I got a friend a job in Records," Constance said to Sally by way of explanation. "It helps to have connections."

The halo chimed. "Monica!" Constance said. "Hey, how's it going?"

They spent a few moments catching up, until finally, Constance got to the point. "Look, I need a favor. Can you run a soul check for me? I need to know where they are."

"Sure!" Monica said. "Who is it?"

"Amaryllis Marian," Constance said. "Amaryllis of House Marian, technically, but same difference. She's got, um… hey, Sal, what's she look like?"

Sally gave her a quick description. "Okay," Constance said, "Brown hair, same eyes, little shorter than me. You can probably rule out the Bad Place, but can't say other than that."

"Just a minute," Monica said. There was a short pause.

"They used to be all scrolls," Constance said as an aside to Sally. "I gave Monica some suggestions and she snuck in a laptop in there. Working on cross-referencing and digitizing the whole bit. Plus they have wi-fi now, which is great."

After the promised minute, which was a lot quicker than the last time Sally had been to Records, Monica came back on the halo. "I've found her," Monica said.

"Great!" Constance said. "Where is she?"

"You're not going to like it," Monica said. "She's in Purgatory. Level Two."

Constance started to say an angry word, but checked herself. "I only get one a year," she muttered. Sally didn't quite understand that. "Why?"

"Level Two is for the envious," Monica said. "Records say it was about someone else, a Lady Eulalie? She learned some other guy had harmed Eulalie, didn't do anything to stop him, watched as he took power, mainly because she wanted the guy and the power for herself. So, yeah, Level Two. Apparently she got murdered by the guy, so-"

"I know the story," Constance sighed. "Thanks, Monica. I owe you." The halo chimed off, leaving just Sally and Constance on the line.

"Okay," Constance said. "So we've got a double pickup to do in Purgatory. Levels Two and Three."

"Wait," Sally said, confused. "We're getting them out? Ourselves? When did we decide to do that?"

"Since you got me involved," Constance said. "That's what I do, Sal. Anyway, so we get them out, and we've got to keep this place safe, and stop your guy Evinrude from murdering people and get him back to the side of good."

"Yeah," Sally said miserably. "I'm not sure we can do all that by ourselves."

"No," Constance said. "We're going to need a third angel. I'd call my superior, Winifred, but this is on the down-low, right?"

"Yeah…" Sally said. "I just, you know, wanted to make things right. You know. On my own."

"Been there," Constance said sympathetically. "Okay. Let me think. Winifred's out, for sure. I could call up Jude, my friend from Virna, but he's up in the ranks, a Principality I think it's called, and he'd have to report in. So he's out. Let me think…well, there's Gilbert."

"Gilbert?" Sally asked. "I don't think I know him."

"Winifred introduced me. Works in the Death Angel Corps. Bit OCD. But, hey, we could use someone in that line." She tapped her halo again. "Hey. Me again. I need Gilbert this time."

"Sorry," an apologetic voice came through. "But it looks like he's got the duty. You know how he hates to be interrupted."

Constance sighed. "Look, just patch me through, would you? This is sort of important. Thanks."

The first thing Gilbert did when he saw the body was to conjure an air freshener and hang it neatly on a tree branch nearby. This wasn't technically standard procedure; as a death angel, his first task was to find the deceased's soul and escort it to its final destination, wherever that happened to be. But Gilbert thoroughly and literally believed that cleanliness was next to godliness, and he hated an untidy scene. Just because one had the misfortune of being dead, he felt, didn't mean one had to leave a mess.

He waited as the pleasant scent of pine needles wafted through the air, calming the smells emanating from the ground. Then, gathering himself and adjusting his halo to the proper angle, Gilbert looked around for the soul. "Ah," he said. "There we are."

The soul was floating, looking a little confused, just above the ground. "Um, am I dead?"

"Yes, 'fraid so," Gilbert said. "Terribly sorry. Looks like we were mauled by a wild animal. A panther, judging by the claw marks. Well, we shouldn't have been wandering out alone in the woods so late, should we?"

"But…" the soul said. "I can't be dead. I had a whole life-"

"Yes, yes, it is tragic," Gilbert said consolingly. He felt he could do this now; he had gotten a good view of the soul and he could see that it was shining clear. Had the soul's color been muddy dark, Gilbert would've let his voice drop into more mournful tones as he prepared to deliver the unwelcome news that the soul was destined for an eternity in the Bad Place. Happily, he didn't have to do that now. "On the bright side," Gilbert said, "While life on Earth has, alas, come to an end, Eternity has only just begun. I've prepared a short presentation on that topic, which I can give now or in pamphlet form to read at leisure." He waited for the soul to say which it wanted.

"I'm dead?" the soul said again.

"Yes," Gilbert said patiently. One had to be patient with the mortals. Still, though, he did have a schedule. "Now, then, happily we've made it to the Blessed Realms of Glory, so we have an appointment with St. Peter at the Pearly Gates. We'd best be making our way there, hadn't we?"

"But-" the soul said.

"Yes, yes, I know," Gilbert said. "No need to worry about the body, it'll be taken care of. Well, let's hurry along then, we wouldn't want to keep St. Peter waiting, would we?" He waved his hand discreetly, and they rose into golden clouds. Soon the soul had been safely ushered into the Pearly Gates, still looking a little bewildered, and Gilbert made a neat little mark on a clipboard. No matter what the more modern angels said, he still preferred a clipboard. It was so much more orderly that way.

Gilbert was just turning back to the clouds for his return to Earth and his next assignment when his halo chimed. "Hello?" he said, a little startled. He thought it was generally understood that he wasn't to be bothered when he had the duty. Interruptions broke up the flow of things.

"Hey," Constance said. "It's me. I need a favor."

Gilbert hesitated. It went against his angelic nature to be impolite, but Constance did have a reputation, one which he knew from experience, having worked with her before. "What sort of favor?" he inquired gingerly.

"No muss, no fuss," Constance said. "Promise. I just need help rescuing two souls from Purgatory."

Gilbert started. "But you can't-"

"Not necessarily," Constance cut in. "I know, once you're in Hell or Heaven you're kinda set, but Purgatory's temporary, right? Meant for purging of sins, right? Okay, so we gotta purge. Look, it's really important, and it'd help a lot. Set some things right, and all that. Okay?"

"Well..." Gilbert looked at his clipboard. The duty was a little light. Also, he had to admit, Constance had been awfully helpful in the incident involving the soul he had misplaced way back in Brooklyn. He did owe her a debt.

"All right," Gilbert said, "Where shall I meet you?"

"Hang on," Constance said. "Forgot the name of the place." There was a momentary chiming of harps. Then Constance came on again. "Loventry. Been there?"

"Yes," Gilbert said distastefully. "Medieval. I shall have to bring wing sanitizer."

"Do that," Constance said. "We're on Isle Turtledove. The beach by the castle. There'll be a big scorch mark on the sand. Can't miss us."

Before Gilbert could inquire about the scorch mark, Constance had chimed off. He gave a sigh and stowed away his clipboard. He was definitely going to need his wing sanitizer, he knew. The last time he had been to Loventry, that world hadn't even invented indoor plumbing yet. For all he knew they still hadn't.

The problem with having a conversation in a forest is that one never knows who might be lurking behind a tree and listening in. While Gilbert was secure on his end before the Pearly Gates, and Sally was safe for the moment in the castle on Isle Turtledove, Constance on the other hand had not thoroughly checked to make sure she was alone before accepting the call on her halo. In her defense, she hadn't quite had the time to conduct a full security sweep given that she was under assault by a very large and very aggravated mother bear.

Still, however, her mistake had consequences. Behind one tree, listening to her conversation, lurked a demon. Although Constance's evil ex-boyfriend Ben was barred from returning to Earth due to his history, some agents from the other side still ventured onto the slowly recovering planet. One of them had overheard the entire conversation, including Sally's explanation of the incident on Loventry, and deemed it significant enough to report.

The report made it down to the Infernal Regions and, due to its significance, wended its way through the diabolical bureaucracy quicker than usual. Constance had somewhat of a reputation down there, and they wanted nothing more than the chance to get even. Soon enough, word had gotten back out again to Leon in Loventry, along with new orders. Not only that, he was also informed that he was to expect reinforcements, and quite a lot of them. The Infernal Regions had decided to make an all-out play for Loventry.

7: Rowena Returns to Loventry

When the lookout atop the crow's nest of the *Paragon* gave the call that land was in view, the sailors sent up a ragged yet heartfelt cry of joy. They were on their fifth captain by now since leaving Kirtle Island. Rowena had torn through the officers' ranks with a vengeance. No one was quite sure who was the captain anymore, and most of the sailors were doing their jobs out of basic training and pure instinct. Fortunately whoever was in charge had managed to accomplish his goal. The *Paragon* came about and made straight for the land, emerging out of the morning fog as the rising sun burned it away. The sailors soon saw that it wasn't just any land; there were buildings, flags, and even the towers of a stout castle looming on a peak. The ship's navigator quickly confirmed what they all suspected. "St. Alexander," he said knowingly. "We're back in Loventry, boys!"

St. Alexander was Loventry's largest port, and under the control of House Brendan. Brendan had fallen in line with Marian and all the other houses behind King Philip and House Shirley, and so Philip's soldiers now walked the streets of the bustling city, making everyone generally on edge. Indeed, even as the *Paragon* approached the dock, a squadron of troops had been drawn up to meet them.

Only then, as the ship put in and the anchor fell, did Rowena emerge from her cabin. She didn't even nod at the officer who had inherited the mantle of ship's captain; she had already forgotten his name. The officer took no offense as she brushed past him and departed, leaving his ship behind, he hoped for good and all. The sailors breathed a collective sigh of relief too. They were now well out of it, they hoped.

She paused just before descending the gangway. "All of you?" she said, raising her voice so the crew and the makeshift captain could hear her. "It would be best if you did not speak of what has happened on this voyage." She left it at that, but they all knew what she meant.

Having said that, Rowena turned and approached the waiting soldiers on the dock. "For me, I presume?" she said.

"Yes, Madam Prime Minister," the captain said respectfully. "King Philip sent us as an escort. What with the trouble on Isle Turtledove and all."

"The trouble where?" Rowena said. She hadn't heard of the latest events, having been preoccupied with her own affairs. As the soldiers fell in around her, forming a protective square, the captain quickly filled her in.

Rowena couldn't quite understand. "A glowing lady drove everyone off the island?"

"Yes, ma'am," the captain said. "Rumor was she was a wizard at first, begging your pardon, but she didn't use lightning bolts or fire or nothing like you all do, just light mostly. Also, the Orders have more or less all said it isn't them."

"Ah," Rowena said. "Even the Polecats?"

The captain snorted. "The Polecats never deny anything, but no one believes 'em anyway. Can't trust a Polecat, y'know,"

"Yes," Rowena said. "Quite." She wondered if the captain would be so glib if he knew how many of the Paragon's officers she'd left in her wake on the voyage home to Loventry. "At any rate, so this, I assume, is why the king has summoned me back."

The captain saluted. "Ma'am. His Majesty awaits your presence at the castle."

"I'm certain he does," Rowena said, scowling. "Fine. Lead on then." She followed the captain as he led her and the soldiers away from the docks and towards the castle on the peak above the town. That, Rowena assumed, was where Philip would be.

She was not wrong. More soldiers met them at the castle doorway, a mixture of men in House Brendan colors and men of Philip's guards. The entire group proceeded inside the castle, a massive block of stone draped in dark green flags; the Brendan lords had a thing for green, apparently. Soon they had arrived at the Great Hall of the castle. The current head of House Brendan, Lord Ryan, stood somewhat awkwardly to the left of the big chair where he plainly was used to sitting himself. In that chair sat Philip, new king of Loventry.

"Took you long enough," he said as Rowena walked in and the doors of the Great Hall closed behind her with a sonorous boom. "Thought you were a wizard. Can't you materialize in the fireplace or something?"

"We don't always," Rowena said frostily. "And if all you wanted me for was my magical abilities, you could've easily summoned another wizard, perhaps one of the Squirrels or the Polecats."

"Perhaps I should summon a Polecat wizard," Philip said. "Know any?"

This brought her up short. She had long suspected that Philip knew her secret, but that he would allude to it so directly in front of the entire court, including Lord Ryan, implied a definite worsening of their relationship. She had thought they were on better terms than that. Rowena shot a rapid glance around the Great Hall; neither Lord Ryan nor any of the guards or courtiers in attendance seemed to have reacted to Philip's question. That was just as well; she wanted to maintain her place as a Rabbit for a little while longer anyway, in name if not in fact. That would give her time to prepare herself for the inevitable retaliation of the Order she had betrayed.

"Not particularly," she said. "They don't run in our circles."

"I didn't think so," Philip said. "I had always understood that the Order of the Rabbit came down particularly hard on Polecats. I've never quite understood the wizards' rules myself. At any rate, we have more pressing concerns." He gestured to a man in armor near the far corner, who stepped forward smartly and saluted. "I've gathered more intelligence on the Isle Turtledove situation from General Evans here. General?"

"Sir," the general said. "We've moved people to watch the island. They don't seem to be doing much. Made no offensive moves across the channel. Mostly they're carrying on as normal."

"But it is *not* normal," Philip said, slamming his fist down on the chair and making everyone in the Great Hall jump. "They have revolted against the rightful authority of the King of Loventry! General, you will gather my armies and prepare for an assault across the channel as soon as practicable. Rowena, you will assist him, along with any other wizards in the service of my house and all the Houses of our kingdom. This assault upon us will not stand!"

The general saluted again. Rowena, rather deliberately, did not salute. "Sir," she said, "Suppose the lady who led the revolt there isn't a wizard? Suppose she relies upon another power, one we do not fully understand?"

"Then I expect you to find a way to understand it and deal with it," Philip said acidly. "Now."

He turned and left the Great Hall. Rowena was shocked. This trifling rebellion seemed to have driven him over the edge. She wondered if something else was going on which she didn't know about. If it was, she decided, she very much needed to know.

It took her surprisingly little time to find out. Being the Prime Minister had given her insights into royal gossip and the intrigues of power in a way she hadn't had before. In this instance, in the immediate aftermath of Philip's departure, she hadn't even made it out of the Great Hall before she was approached by Lord Ryan. "Madam Prime Minister," he began. "Might I have a word?"

Rowena hesitated. Philip's guards, ostensibly for her protection, were still drawn up nearby. She wasn't entirely sure where everyone's loyalties were. "I'm afraid I have some pressing matters to attend to, as you no doubt observed," she said cautiously. "If this involves something serious…"

"Oh, no, nothing like that," Lord Ryan said. "As it happens, I've arranged for you and His Majesty to dine with me and Lady Caroline tonight, along with some others, and perhaps then we might discuss it. I assure you, it involves no pressing matter." He made a gracious bow and departed.

Rowena was left to ponder this as the guards escorted her to her quarters in the castle. Perhaps Lord Ryan really did have only a minor matter to discuss with her; if that were the case, no harm done. On the other hand, although Rowena was relatively new to the world of power politics, she wasn't a complete novice; one didn't approach the prime minister in a moment of crisis over a minor thing. If it were that inconsequential, he would've just come right out and made his request. Also, a private conversation could still be had at a dinner, depending on the seating arrangement. If she were seated between Ryan and Caroline, and Philip was distracted by Caroline, Ryan would make his request to her without Philip hearing, or perhaps arrange another more private meeting.

The question, of course, was what he really wanted? Was he loyal to Philip and looking to sound out her own loyalty? Or was he hoping to stir up a revolt, taking advantage of House Turtledove's defiance, and seeing if she might be willing to break ranks too? He had given no clear indication either way.

Rowena considered the matter all afternoon, idly preparing death curses as she did so, just in case something happened. Outside her room, Philip's guards stood at her doorway, supposedly to protect her from intruders. Beyond the castle, on the docks, the sailors of the ship *Paragon* had finished loading up the vessel with cargo, as their newest captain had taken the opportunity to make a deal with a local merchant to transport his goods to another port, with a handsome profit for the captain and crew involved. The sailors were relieved, as they now assumed they would be out of Loventry and away from Rowena and her terrifying moods and random murders.

The captain was just about to give the order to cast off the lines and set sail when a man hailed him from the dock. "Captain Jenkins?"

"Oh, no," the captain said, a little embarrassed, "Sorry, I'm, erm, McFilby. Captain McFilby."

The man looked rather dramatically at a list he held in his hand. "McFilby? I didn't know they still had Fifth Mates in the Loventry merchant service anymore. And you're the captain now? You're a bit down on the chain of command, aren't you?" As he spoke, he casually walked up the gangplank, his face not quite visible in the flaring lamplight overhead.

"We had a bit of trouble on the way in," McFilby said, irritated now. "And we're on our way out, actually, so unless you have business here-"

"I do," the man said, and suddenly his voice changed, and was no longer casual. "I know all about your trouble. It seems very unfair. Four of your officers murdered. You left in charge by default. Your ship commandeered. And with no recompense for you or your crew?"

Suspicious as McFilby was, and McFilby already had his hand on his sword, he had to admit the man had a point. "But she's the bloomin' Prime Minister," he said. "I can't just go and complain about her!"

"Can't you?" the man said. "She's a wizard, isn't she? In the Rabbit order? I thought Rabbits had rules."

"Oh," said McFilby. He hadn't thought of that. "But what if she-"

"And," the man said. "If you don't complain, and ally yourself with some good wizards now for your protection, she might decide later to cover it up. You can imagine what that means. Particularly if she's gone bad and joined the Polecats. Think about it." With that, he turned and walked abruptly back down the gangplank and into the gathering night.

McFilby didn't have to think very long. Soon he was hurrying off into the darkness. Evinrude watched him go. "Now," he said to Leon standing beside him, "to the castle."

The wizard community in Loventry was somewhat loosely organized. The various orders, unlike the mercenary fraternity for example, did not have a centralized headquarters or a single magical tower at which they congregated to practice spells or exchange wizard gossip. At the most, what they had in some of the larger cities were various houses set aside especially for them, with rooms and the promise of a good fire and a meal. At these houses some of the more established Orders had taken to setting up offices for anyone needing their services.

Thus it was that McFilby arrived at the St. Alexander Rabbit house later that night and knocked fearfully on the door. It swung readily open, and he was met by a burst of warm light and song. When his eyes got used to the light, he found he was looking into a large common room in which a number of Rabbit wizards were having a rousing drinking party and were well on their way to getting thoroughly plastered. "Oi, there!" one called to McFilby. "C'mon in, join the fun!"

"Sorry," McFilby said, a little diffidently, "I'm not a wizard, you see, I've actually come to make a complaint about one of the members of the, ah, Rabbit order. I'd like compensation, y'see…"

He was drowned out as the Rabbit wizard, having lost interest half a sentence ago, had turned back to the song. So had most of the other wizards, many of whom hadn't even noticed McFilby's arrival.

One wizard in the corner had seen him, however. The wizard rose from his chair and quietly approached McFilby. "Hello," he said calmly. "I'm Peter. I'm the designated Order representative for the evening, in case something like this comes up. I'm perfectly sober. Haven't had a drink all week. You said you had a complaint about one of the members of our Order?"

Very much relieved, McFilby poured out his tale of woe. As he spoke, Peter's face grew steadily dark. "I see," he said at last. "This is serious, as you can imagine. Very serious."

"Yeah," McFilby said. "You're telling me. Four captains we lost!"

"Indeed. I'll have to take it up with the Rabbit High Council."

Peter saw the look of skepticism on McFilby's face and guessed at his disappointment. "Oh, don't worry," he said. "This isn't going to get lost in a tangle of discussion and meetings somewhere. We will do something about this. You have our word."

His wand, which McFilby hadn't noticed before, flashed in his hand. McFilby, who hadn't quite believed him before, believed him now. "That's just what I wanted," he said nervously. "That's all I wanted, really. Something to be done about it. I'll just go back to the ship and wait, then, shall I?"

"Yes," Peter said. "Do that."

Once McFilby had gone, Peter acted quickly. He administered a rapid sobering-up spell to the next Rabbit wizard in line, one Bill, who was none too pleased; a magical sobering up is not a pleasant experience. "You're going to have to look after things for a bit," Peter said. "I've got to call the High Council."

"That important, is it?" Bill said.

"Oh, yes," Peter said, "It is that important."

Next Peter withdrew to a private chamber in the Rabbit house which held a plain mirror, unadorned with a simple wooden frame. Some wizards decorated their magical mirrors beyond all reason, with fancy golden frames and wildly carved stands. The Rabbit philosophy was that this attracted unwanted attention. If one had the good fortune to possess a magical mirror, one had best keep the thing secret so no one else would find it. Without knowing its true nature, a passer-by might just as easily take the opportunity to check their reflection in the mirror and then walk on, unaware. That was perfectly fine with the Rabbit wizards.

Peter, of course, being a Rabbit wizard himself, knew better. He stepped to the mirror and tapped the bottom edge with his wand. "Hello," he said. "I'd like to speak with the High Council. It's very important."

This took some setting up. One couldn't just tap the magic mirror and expect the nine grand wizards of the Rabbit High Council to appear instantaneously in the frame on command. The mirror sparkled and buzzed for a moment or two, and then filled with nine pictures of the wizards' various assistants, some of them looking like they had just emerged from their beds, which of course they had. After Peter had explained who he was and given his credentials, the secretaries went to fetch their superiors. A few moments later, their pictures were replaced by the pictures of the Rabbit High Council, all except for one on the lower left, which had dissolved in grey. The wizard in the middle square coughed gently. "Adalbert, can you hear me?"

"Of course I can hear you, Egmond," an irate voice said. "You can hear me, can't you? I'm not an idiot, I know how to work these things!"

"We can't see you though," the center wizard said patiently. "You remember, you need to tap the bottom edge twice with your wand."

"Of course I remember!" the voice said. There was a slight tap, and the lower left square resolved into the picture of a scowling man in a nightcap and grey flannel. "Now, what's all this about?"

Peter was about to explain when they heard a sudden clanging roar, followed by a distinctly childlike shriek. The woman in the upper right corner winced. "Sorry," she explained. "My littlest brought home a baby Twisty-Bottomed Spittuck from magic school and she's trying to train it."

Egmond, in his central square, sighed wearily. "May I remind the council once again to please silence your magical mirrors if you are not the one speaking? Thank you. Now then, Peter?"

Peter explained what McFilby had told him. There was a long silence. "Have you verified the man's accusations yet?" Egmond asked.

"No, sir," Peter said. "I thought it best to bring this matter straight to the Council first, given the nature."

"You did right," Egmond said. "An accusation against the Prime Minister is not to be taken lightly."

"Indeed so, sir," Peter said. He paused delicately. "May I then proceed to look into the allegations? If they are true-"

"Then it would mean that one of our order has committed foul murder!" Adalbert interrupted. "Such a thing would be unconscionable!"

"It would," Egmond said, "If it is true. And even if it is, we work in perilous times. Rowena is second in command to Philip, and we have long suspected he has alliances with the Polecats. If we cast her out, do we risk open war with him?"

The council fell silent. "Sir?" Peter said. "What should I do about McFilby? I gave him my word."

"You did, didn't you," Egmond said. "Right. You'd better look into it. Before we do anything else, we need to know if this is true. Go back to the ship, talk to the men. Then you should probably go to Kirtle Island and find out what happened there. Try not to use magical transport unless you have to; you never know who might be watching the ways."

"I do keep track of my socks, you know, sir," Peter said defensively."

"Yes, that's what everyone says," Egmond said. "Until a sock is lost. Best to go by ship anyway. Follow the track. And be careful."

"Yes, sir," Peter said, saluting with his wand.

He turned to go. Behind him, he heard a few of the wizards muttering. "He'll probably get himself killed, he will."

"I heard that," Peter said.

Egmond scowled. "Again, must I remind the council to close out your mirrors when a meeting is over? Please?"

The dinner in the castle of House Brendan that night was well put on, with laden tables and drinks all around for anyone who wanted them. When Lord Ryan had mentioned that some others would be dining with Lady Caroline and Rowena, he had slightly under-exaggerated. The dining hall of the castle was full of courtiers, not to mention a thorough roster of the top ranks of Philip's soldiers. At first Rowena was annoyed when she walked into the dining hall and saw the crowd. Then a servant ushered her to her seat, with Ryan on her left, Caroline on her right, and Philip on Caroline's right, and she realized that the general din of conversation in the hall would make it impossible for anyone, especially the king, to hear what Lord Ryan said to her, if he spoke carefully. Her estimation of him rose fractionally. She was also more wary; if he was putting this much thought into it, he must have something extraordinarily important to discuss.

During the first course he didn't say much at all. Lady Caroline carried the conversation, introducing utterly uninteresting topics such as the weather (it was lovely for the time of year), the dinner ("try this cordial, it's divine!"), and everyone's health (Lord Roger of House Duffield over there had a cold, the poor dear). While Rowena was taken up with her, Lord Ryan was in conversation with the person on his left, a general in Philip's army. From what Rowena could tell, they were discussing the impending assault upon Isle Turtledove. Forces were moving into place, but the wizards allied to House Shirley seemed curiously reluctant to lend their assistance. Rowena made a mental note to make some inquiries into that, when she had a chance. If Philip's support was weakening in one quarter, it might well be weakening in others.

At last, as the main course arrived and the buzz of conversation rose, Lady Caroline drifted into conversation with Philip, and Lord Ryan finally appeared to remember that Rowena was on his right. "So, Prime Minister," he said, "How do you find the castle?"

"Interesting," Rowena said cautiously. Interesting, she had always found, was such a delightfully value-neutral word. "Of course, I've been in the islands for a little while, and I'm somewhat more comfortable there than on land."

"Indeed," Lord Ryan said. "I'd heard you lived on Kirtle Island before you assumed your present post. I wonder, talking of islands, have you ever been to Isle Turtledove?"

Rowena sensed they were coming to the point. She took a slight drink from her wineglass to calm her nerves. "No," she said. "I haven't. Have you?" Rowena was rather pleased with her quick turning back of the conversation upon Lord Ryan. Was he skilled enough to parry the blow?

Lord Ryan shrugged. "Twice," he said calmly. "Some years ago, for my sister-in-law's marriage. After that, for the birth of their child, a girl." It took Rowena a second for this to register. All at once she saw that Lady Caroline had broken from the conversation with Philip and had fixed her eyes on Rowena.

"We never had a daughter of our own," Lady Caroline said, steel in her voice. "When my sister had Eulalie, I loved her. I thought she had my eyes. I never quite understood what happened to her. Dragons don't just attack people out of nowhere. Then I came into some information recently."

Rowena tensed, her hand cautiously going towards her wand. "What sort of information?"

"Information about your family," Caroline said. "Your true family. Incidentally, how do you find your cordial?"

Rowena was a little disoriented by the abrupt subject change. She looked down at her glass, which by then was empty. It blurred in her hand. She realized that her disorientation wasn't going away. Rowena, too late, began to conjure a death curse, but already the room was darkening around her.

"But…" she managed. "But I didn't…I didn't…"

"Of course you did," Lady Caroline said. "You're a Polecat. It's what you do."

It was the last thing Rowena heard as a mortal.

When the darkness lifted, she saw a pair of iron gates before her. Leon stood beside them, smirking. "Hiya," he said. "Y'know, I wasn't sure who was gonna pull this. And honestly you might've gotten off with Purgatory except for the murders. That got you Circle Seven."

"Circle…" Rowena blinked. Then she realized that she could see through her eyelids. "What? Am I-"

"Dead? Like, yeah," Leon said. "You got poisoned, genius. See, Evinrude knows. He knows about your dad, knows about how you helped Phil, everything. And so he cut a deal with me to get vengeance. Looked up family relations, got you back to St. Alexander. You know, the best part was when we told Ryan and Caroline that you were the one that killed off their daughter on Philip's orders. They couldn't go after him, he's got too many guys, too many dragons, but you? You're just one little scheming wizard! You're easy!"

Leon giggled nastily. "Anyway, I've got to get back to Loventry, big things going on there, vengeance and war and all that. You got this, Nessie?"

"I've asked you not to call me that," rumbled a deep voice from inside the gates. "I am Nessus, guardian of Phlegethon, river of fire. My name is *not* Nessie."

Leon chortled. "Right, right, yeah. Anyhow. See ya!" He disappeared in flame. The gates swung open. Rowena vanished into them, forever.

Meanwhile, back in St. Alexander, the dining hall had erupted into tumult. Doctors had been fetched, to no avail. King Philip demanded to know what had happened. Lord Ryan, apparently grief-stricken, couldn't imagine. "We were just talking and then she fell!"

In the chaos of the moment, no one noticed that Lady Caroline had exchanged a look with one of the servants. He nodded back and left, a small smile on his face. "Scratch one," Evinrude said quietly. "Scratch one."

8: The Unwilling Rescued

When Gilbert arrived on the beach at Isle Turtledove on the morning after Rowena's death, he hadn't expected the beach to be deserted exactly. He knew this wouldn't be a modern beach with sunbathers and surfboarders, but he had expected a few people to be around looking for shells and enjoying the sea breeze, possibly trying to catch a fish or two. Also, he made it a matter of course when arriving anywhere in the mortal world to do so invisibly, just in case, as you never knew when one of the humans might be looking your way.

He was glad he did so, for what he did not expect was to find the beach he popped in on to be under observation by an entire army across the channel. The moment he touched sand, he felt the swoosh of a dragon's wings overhead. Across the waves, he saw massive griffins lumbering across another beach parallel to his own, accompanied by rows of armored guards.

"Lovely, aren't they," Constance said dryly, materializing next to him. "They've been doing that for a day or two now. More all the time. Kinda upset this morning, seems like. Not sure why."

Indeed, the dragons circling overhead were roaring a bit more loudly than they usually did. "I imagine they'll probably attack in a bit," Constance said casually. "Sally, you cool handling this?"

"Um…" Sally said.

"Great!" Constance said. "We'll be in Purgatory if you need us. Bye!" With that, she waved, and both she and Gilbert vanished, before Gilbert even had time to apply his wing sanitizer. Sally gulped as yet another dragon soared overhead. This was yet again getting to be a bit beyond her.

The speedboat cut through the waves, its white prow knifing through the surf as spray flashed out behind. Gilbert clung to the edges of the boat, eyes closed fast. "Couldn't we just fly there?" he pleaded. "You're not supposed to approach the gates of Purgatory in a speedboat! It's not good form!"

"But what would be the fun?" Constance said, revving up the boat to go even faster as they sped past the Rock of Gibraltar. "Look, we had to come all the way back to Earth to get to the gates to this place, we might as well enjoy ourselves, y'know?"

Gilbert didn't look like he agreed. Constance was still relatively new as an angel, although she was learning; it occurred to her that she had never had occasion to ask whether an angel could become seasick. Fortunately at that moment a massive grey mountain loomed in view over the horizon.

"Ah," said Gilbert in visible relief, "There it is. The Mountain of Purgatory."

"Yep, there it is," Constance said, slowing the boat. "Hey, how come none of the humans ever noticed a great big old mountain sitting out in the ocean before? You think they would've."

"The Mountain of Purgatory is invisible," Gilbert said. "Obviously."

"Right," Constance said, rolling her eyes. "Duh. Silly me."

"What I mean is," Gilbert said patiently, "it doesn't exist in the mortal realm, accessible to humans, any more than Hell does. It is visible to us now because we are angels. We exist in realms spiritual."

"Right," Constance said. "I knew that."

At that moment, the boat scudded to a stop in grey sand. Gilbert stepped out carefully and tied the boat fast to a slim willow nearby. Constance was already dashing up a nearby path. "C'mon, buddy, time's wasting!" she called.

"And if the boat floats away?" Gilbert said. "One must always make sure!"

"Did you forget the part where we can fly?" Constance reminded him as he started after her. "Also, I can always snap up another one."

"Waste of effort, when we still have the one," Gilbert said. "And let's keep our voice down, shall we? We're not exactly alone."

"I don't see anyone," Constance said, as they rounded a turn in the path into a low valley. At the end of the valley rose a flight of grey steps that ended in a massive gateway, barred with mighty doors. "Besides, we're angels. Who's gonna-"

At that moment, a blinding light blasted in their faces. "Bigger angels," Gilbert said, and dropped to one knee, motioning for Constance to get down beside him. "Much bigger angels."

"*Who approaches the gate of Purgatory?*" a resounding voice boomed over them.

"O mighty guardian of the gates," Gilbert began, "We respectfully-"

"Boris?" Constance interrupted. She bounded up from the ground, laughing. "Boris, is that you? Hey, how've you been?"

"*I have told you, my name is not Boris!*" growled the angel.

"Yeah, yeah, I know, it's something unpronounceable in earthly tongues, blah blah blah," Constance said. "It's got a *Bor* and an *is* in there somewhere, so close enough!"

"You know him?" Gilbert said, astounded. "You know the angel that guards the gates of Purgatory?"

"Yeah," Constance said. "Through a friend. He's looking after the Ten Commandments now. Long story. Anyway. Look, Boris, buddy, we need to get in Purgatory, rescue some people, so help us out, would you?"

"*I cannot,*" Boris said, scowling. "*It is my duty to guard the gates of Purgatory, bearing eternally this great sword that I wield.*" He hefted it so they could see. The blade reached high over his head and shone with a dazzling light. Constance was duly impressed.

"Cool," she said. "But we're not asking you to let down your guard. Just to let us go through and break some other people out."

"*No one leaves Purgatory before their time!*" Boris said, his mighty eyebrows arched.

"Of course not," Constance said. "We'll just be going then." She turned away, her wings slumped. Then she leaned over and whispered quickly to Gilbert, "Hey, can I borrow some of that wing sanitizer you have?"

Gilbert handed her a bottle. "Just remember," he began, "two pumps per wing, and make sure to give the pinions a thorough-"

But Constance had already spun around and thrown the bottle straight at Boris, then snapped her fingers. The bottle of wing sanitizer, a curious blend of manmade and heavenly chemicals, ignited in blinding fire. Even Boris reeled back in alarm. "Run!" Constance yelled, and dived past the guardian angel. Gilbert, shocked by her audacity, had enough presence of mind to follow. The two angels ran up the steps, through the gateway, and into Purgatory itself. Constance whirled and slammed the doors shut behind them. She heard a mighty *clong*, which sounded very much as if someone on the other side had struck the gates with a gigantic sword. This, of course, was exactly what had happened. Fortunately, the gates of Purgatory were as unyielding as the gates of Hell.

While Boris clanged against the gates behind them, Gilbert and Constance took a moment to regroup and look around. They stood in a narrow crevice of rock which opened out onto a terrace that curved away to the right. Constance moved cautiously out onto the terrace, Gilbert following even more cautiously. On their left, the terrace fell away in a steep drop, the waves of the sea thundering endlessly below. On their right, a shining white wall rose, adorned with marble carvings. Gilbert paused to make out what they were, as the carvings were quite artistically done, but Constance hurried on. "C'mon," she called back over her shoulder. "Someone's going to hear us any minute!"

She whipped around the corner, and Gilbert heard a distinct *thud,* followed by a plaintive "Ow…" It didn't sound like an outraged cry, however, or even a cry of pain, it almost sounded apologetic, as if the person crying out was apologizing for the trouble of the disturbance. Gilbert hurried around the corner, where Constance stood aghast before the soul of an older man who had apparently dropped a very large rock on his foot. "You okay?" Constance was saying, forgetting in her upset that the man was dead and therefore by definition beyond mortal terms of okay or not okay. "I didn't mean to do that, honest-"

"It's all right," the man said meekly, "It's not a very big rock. It could've happened to anyone really."

"Could've happened…" Constance spluttered. "Dude! I just made you drop this massive boulder on your foot! I know you're not really alive anymore but come on! You're not mad?"

"Oh no," the man said. "That would be the vice of wrath, which would be the third level of purgatory. I'm not nearly important enough for that yet."

"Uh-huh," Constance said. "And this level would be…"

"Pride," Gilbert said. Out of sheer habit the angel checked his clipboard. Miraculously the relevant papers appeared. "We appear to have thirty years left in our time here."

"We?"

"He does," Gilbert said, gesturing to the man. "You and I should be moving on to Level Two."

"Right," Constance said. "Let's do that. Sorry, pal."

"Not at all," the man said. "Come again sometime! A pleasure meeting you!" He actually sounded as if he meant it. Constance didn't understand him at all.

They kept on running, past more souls carrying their load of large rocks unendingly down the terrace past them, until the two angels reached a flight of steps that cut into a crevice into the mountainside. "Ah," Gilbert said, "That'll take us to Level Two. I believe you said the first soul you wanted was here?"

"Yeah," Constance said as they climbed up the steps, "Amaryllis. She's in for envy. What's the deal for envious people here?"

"Well," Gilbert said, "It used to be that their eyes were sewn shut with iron wire, but-"

"Yikes," Constance said.

"Precisely. I found it a bit distasteful when I joined the Death Angel Corps, so I made a few recommendations," Gilbert said modestly.

"So what is it now?"

They came out of the crevice and emerged onto a new terrace, and Constance saw a new line of people shuffling past. She gasped, trying to stifle a giggle. "*Sunglasses?*"

"Well, it's better than iron wire," Gilbert said. "And they can't see out of them anyway, so it comes to the same thing. Also, with a proper washing, you can reuse them once the soul moves on to higher realms. It's a bit difficult to do that with iron wire sewn into the eyes. Not nearly as hygienic, you know."

"Right," Constance said. "Sure, yeah. Okay, so we're looking for Amaryllis. Brown hair, forget her eye color, wouldn't matter anyway because of the sunglasses. She's about yay-high, and she was super jealous of Eulalie because Eulalie stole her guy. She's not in the Bad Place because, erm, well, actually the finer points of that escape me, but you probably get that more than I do."

"Well, actually," Gilbert began to explain.

"Shut it," Constance said irritably. "Just help me look."

The two angels ran swiftly down the line of sunglass-wearing penitents, stopping at everyone with brown hair to check if she might be Amaryllis. After about an hour, even their angelic energy began to flag. "How many people are *in* here?" Constance said.

"It depends," Gilbert said. "People come, people go. It's not a fixed point, you know. One is supposed to move on, eventually."

It occurred to Constance then that she hadn't checked to see if anyone might have been offering prayers for Amaryllis's soul back in Loventry. If that had happened, Amaryllis might have already moved on to Heaven, in which case it would be a lot more difficult to convince her to return to mortal life and marry Evinrude. Constance was just about to tap her halo and ask for Monica in Records to double-check where Amaryllis was when they rounded another corner in the terrace, and she collided with another soul. "I'm so sorry," she apologized, "Again. I'm just not getting the hang of this place!"

"Who's there?" the soul said, backing away in alarm. "Who're you?"

Constance considered explaining, but then decided it would take too long. "We're angels, just passing through. Hey, you wouldn't know a girl named Amaryllis, would you?"

"Actually, that's me," the soul said. "My name is Amaryllis of House Marian. What do you want?" She backed nervously up against the white wall of the terrace. Constance could see her brown hair now, behind her dark sunglasses, and underneath a grey cloak, she thought she saw a ghostly scar as if left behind by an arrow.

"Well," Constance said brightly, "We've come to rescue you!"

"You've come to what?" Amaryllis said.

"We've come to retrieve you from Purgatory and take you back to Loventry so Evinrude can marry you and set everything right again!" Constance explained.

She had assumed Amaryllis would be reasonably happy to be rescued, as anyone would be. Purgatory wasn't Hell, exactly, but neither was it Heaven; as Gilbert had previously pointed out, no one wanted to stay there. What Constance did not expect was for Amaryllis to pull back and smack her right in the face. Constance being an angel, this didn't hurt her at all, but it shocked her very much. "What the-"

"Language!" Gilbert cut in.

"Not you too!" Constance said, rolling her eyes. "I know, okay, we're angels, we have a policy, and I worked it all out with Winifred, I get one word a year. Besides, she smacked me! Me, when I'm trying to rescue her!"

"Did you ask whether I want to be rescued?" Amaryllis demanded. "Especially if you're going to make me marry that wretched rat- " Here she unleashed a torrent of frightfully descriptive words that scandalized even Constance and caused Gilbert to clap his hands over his ears. "Anyway," she concluded, "I refuse. I will not marry him. I would rather stay here. For eternity."

With that, Amaryllis turned on her heel and stormed away, following the line of penitent sunglasses-wearing souls down the terrace.

"No kidding," Constance said dryly. "Gilbert, you can unplug your ears now, she's done."

"Thank you," the angel said, relieved. "I hesitate to point out that this does present a bit of a problem for our plan."

Consider sighed. "We'll improvise."

Gilbert winced. "I dislike improvisation. It never works well. Some years ago, when I was in the Messenger Corps, I was sent to tell a man and his wife that they were going to have a child. He asked me what my name was. I didn't want to tell him it was Gilbert, which hardly seemed to fit the moment, so I improvised. I said that it was a thing of wonder. I meant to imply that it was not for human ears. Somehow he ... misheard."

"Yeah...?" Constance said.

"Well, when the child grew up, he was gifted with enormous strength, only with the condition that if he cut his hair, he would lose his strength. Test of devotion, you know. Well, one night he fell into trouble with a young lady. His father had a bad feeling that night and sent up a prayer. By then I'd been assigned to be the child's guardian, and I should've been on hand to help, but the man addressed his plea to an angel named Wanda. By the time the mistake was sorted out and everyone realized it was me they wanted..." Gilbert shrugged. "Well, you know the rest."

Constance gasped. "Samson? That was you? Yikes."

"Yes," Gilbert said miserably. "That was me. How was I to know?"

"Still, though," Constance said, "Epic guy. Killed a thousand soldiers with the jawbone of a donkey, yeah?"

"Yes," Gilbert said. "Not my preferred weapon, but yes."

"How'd he do that anyway? They stand in line or what?"

"It's complicated," Gilbert said delicately. "With enough force and at just the right angles, and if you allow for some rounding in the precise numbers..." he paused. "Setting that aside for the moment, what do you suggest we do now? We could still attempt a recovery of the other soul, Eulalie?"

"No," Constance said, clenching her fist. Her halo flashed above her head. "We're not leaving Amaryllis behind. I'm going to drag her out of Purgatory by force if I have to."

"I'm not sure you can do that-" Gilbert began.

"Watch me."

With that, she launched herself into the air and shot away down the terrace. In a moment she was back, dragging a screaming Amaryllis by her arm. "Let go!" Amaryllis howled. "I'm not going back! Not ever!"

"We'd best get to Level Three *fast*," Constance said quickly to Gilbert as she swooped low over his head. "I don't think we'll be alone for long!" Gilbert could only extend his wings and follow after.

The two angels, with a flailing Amaryllis in tow, whipped down the second terrace of Purgatory as fast as their wings could carry them, which, considering they were angels, was considerably fast. They flashed around one corner, and then another, and then careened up a crevice and another flight of steps, and found themselves blasting out into a billowing cloud of acrid smoke. Constance whirled and snapped her fingers at the doorway, which instantly congealed into a wall of solid rock. "That should slow 'em down," she said.

"You do realize they're angels too?" Gilbert said.

"Right," Constance said. "Well, anyway, let's just grab Eulalie and go, okay?"

Gilbert looked down at his clipboard, just out of habit. A thought occurred to him, and rather than ask Constance to go through her friend in Records, he decided to do it himself. Gilbert tapped the clipboard, and it flashed golden, miraculously displaying the papers relevant to Eulalie's location. Gilbert smiled at first; as usual, the old ways worked just fine, thank you. Then his smile faded as he read the papers. "Ah, Constance?" he said. "We have a problem. She's not here anymore."

"What?" Constance said. "What do you mean? How do you-"

The angel gestured to his clipboard. "Evidently the prayers Sally started back on Isle Turtledove worked," Gilbert said. "She's worked through the wrath problem. Having done that and purged her sin, she has moved on."

"So what level is she on now?" Constance said.

There was a long pause. "Oh no."

"Yes," Gilbert said. "Wrath was the primary vice from which she needed to be cleansed. Once she addressed that, she would have been able to ascend up to Heaven."

"Is she there yet?"

"What?"

"*Is she there yet?*" Constance pressed.

Gilbert looked down at his clipboard and gave it a quick tap. "Well, it doesn't seem like she's quite-"

"Come on!" Constance yelled, and she shot away, light flashing and Amaryllis screaming in her wake. There was nothing left for Gilbert to do but follow her into the smoke of Level Three.

9: The Battle of Isle Turtledove

Back on Isle Turtledove, Sally was pacing back and forth nervously on the beach where Lady Eulalie had died, watching as the forces of King Philip gathered their strength on the opposite shore. She still wasn't sure what to do.

Sally had her hand on the hilt of her sword, but she hesitated to draw it. She had never actually used it in deliberate anger. She hadn't even used it when she had driven the soldiers from Isle Turtledove; that had been pure split-second reaction, nothing more. After all, she wasn't part of the Archangel Michael's official Battle Brigades; those were angels specially qualified to wage eternal war against the forces of darkness. She was just one lonely angel with a sword, facing down a mighty host of dragons, griffins, and men with a great many swords of their own, not to mention arrows, spears, and other nasty pointed things. What was she supposed to do?

She had at least managed to get the innocent people secure, for the moment. Everyone was holed up in the castle with supplies Sally had miraculously waved into being, and the people were now all waiting on her to accomplish their deliverance. Eulalie's parents didn't seem quite as confident in this as the ordinary folk, but Sally had assured them that very morning that she had the situation well in hand. Now, however, as she stood on the sand watching the gathering horde, she wasn't quite so sure.

Just then one of the dragons buzzed the beach, swooping uncomfortably low over her head and roaring loudly. They had been doing that a lot lately, being increasingly more aggressive. Sally wondered if she should throw something at it. Then she saw the dragon turn, and realized it was about to make another pass. For the first time since the death of Father Thomas, the island's original chaplain, Sally lost her temper. "Back off!" she snapped, and waved her hand towards the dragon. "Now!"

The air cracked with thunder. The dragon reeled back in alarm. Black clouds materialized overhead. Hail lashed at the channel. Before Sally realized what was happening, an all-out thunderstorm had broken out over the island, unparalleled in its fury. Lightning tore across the sky, striking at the army on the opposite shore and sending the soldiers scurrying for cover. Sally cringed. She hadn't meant to call down a thunderstorm.

She waved gingerly at the storm, hoping to settle it down so that it wouldn't be too destructive; the last thing Sally wanted was to smite both the army and Isle Turtledove alike. The storm grudgingly subsided into a steady pouring rain, cold and miserable, the kind that seeped into clothes and thoroughly drenched whoever was out in it. It also made all the roads in the area completely muddy and impassable, and reduced air visibility to near zero, which had the happy effect of stalling the battle. Sally decided she could live with that and went back inside the castle.

The rain kept on falling. Constance and Gilbert were away in Purgatory on their pursuit of Amaryllis. Peter, the Rabbit wizard, was sailing for Kirtle Island, determined to uncover the truth about Rowena's activities, unaware as of yet that she had already been murdered. Leon sloshed around in the mud on the shore opposite Isle Turtledove, wondering when the rain would stop and trying not to get stepped on by a dragon or some other monster. This was getting harder and harder to do, as there were getting to be more and more of them. Leon didn't even know where they were all coming from. He had tried to scare off the Polecat wizards, and thought he had succeeded in doing this to most of them, but even so, the dragons and griffins kept coming. Leon kept sloshing around and trying not to get stepped on, and the army kept growing regardless.

Philip himself had left such matters as the army to his generals and wizards, as he had left the entire problem of the rebellious little island. He had moved on to higher affairs. He didn't believe that Rowena had dropped dead of her own accord for a moment. Philip had already ordered Lord Ryan and Lady Caroline arrested and clapped in the darkest dungeon in St. Alexander, pending a trial which he had no intention of ever letting happen. What worried him wasn't so much their act of treachery; they had done him a favor, in a sense, by getting rid of Rowena. Philip had long been concerned about her true loyalty, and now he didn't have to worry anymore.

What troubled him was what their betrayal signaled about the rest of the Loventry royal houses. Philip had thought House Brendan was solidly in his corner; he couldn't understand why they would've broken away. They couldn't possibly have found out about his murders of Eulalie and Amaryllis; he had that secret all sewn up.

On the other hand, if they didn't know his secret and had still gone so far in rebellion as to assassinate his Prime Minister, what about the others? He had to do something to ensure that the rest didn't dare turn against him. He couldn't try marrying and murdering another noble lady again like Amaryllis; that trick only worked so often before people began to catch on. There remained only the old standby. He was going to have to take Loventry to war.

Once Philip had made that decision, the rest fell into place easily. First he needed a target. He had already narrowed it down to Ilariana or Seyna; now he decided on the southern kingdom Ilariana. Besides its strategic importance to trade routes, he also knew that the Mercenary Guild made its headquarters there. Philip had made use of its services a time or two in the past, including arranging the murder of Amaryllis. This would be the opportunity to make sure they would never be able to reveal that particular incident, and as a happy side effect, to head off a potential threat they might pose to his long-term power. Seyna he could deal with later. All he needed now was a cause. Philip mulled over that as he made his preparations while the rain fell on.

Outside the castle of House Brendan, alone in the dark and the rain, Evinrude stood shrouded in the cloak of disguise he had stolen from the late Mortimer. He knew Philip had to be getting nervous. The nobility were restless, his wizard support had faltered (or so Leon had assured him), and now his prime minister was gone. Philip still had his army, however, and that was no small thing. That was next on Evinrude's list, and he already had plans to deal with that. He stared down at his sword, watching as the raindrops slid down the blade.

The rain kept on falling for the next several days. The army began to grow restive. Finally, Philip, distracted as he was with his preparations for a war against Ilariana, lost patience. The one thing he could not afford was to leave a rebellious family like House

Turtledove unattended to in his rear while he marched away south. He had to attack, and that meant he had to deal with the rain.

In the old days he would've approached Alistair and asked him to do a bit of Polecat magic. Unfortunately Alistair had gone missing and the messenger ravens Philip had sent after the wizard had yet to return. Ever since then he'd had no small end of trouble making contact with the Polecat wizards on his family's payroll. Pacing back and forth in the throne room of House Brendan's castle, Philip finally snapped. "Fine, then," he said to no one in particular. "We attack!"

"Milord?" a passing servant said, caught off guard.

Philip jerked in surprise, having overlooked the servant's presence. "Call my generals," he said brusquely. "Evans and all the rest of them. Now."

The servant had no idea how to do this. She was a random scullery maid, tasked to scrub floors and clean fireplaces. Through no fault of her own, she didn't even know how to contact the lowliest private in Philip's army, let alone his top military leaders. In desperation she went to the kitchen maid to whom she reported. That worthy individual, equally flummoxed, went to the cook, who then went to the housekeeper. Under normal circumstances she would've taken her concerns up the chain of command to the butler, but in this instance she had a shortcut. The housekeeper had taken up with a general on the quiet, having met the man on her night off while she was having a drink at a portside bar. She therefore skipped the butler and went straight to her general friend, who immediately summoned the other generals. Horses tore out into the rain, messengers went running, and within the hour Philip's entire military staff had assembled in the king's council chamber, which he had commandeered from Lord Ryan.

"What took you so long?" the king snapped at his top commander, ignorant of the herculean efforts that had gone into carrying out his orders.

"Sir?" General Evans said. Evans was a careful man, attentive to protocol, low-risk. He had worked his way up stolidly through the ranks of the royal army, such as it had been, and he was uncomfortable with all the new additions of dragons and griffins that seemed to be flooding in from who knew where. That said, he remained loyal to Loventry and its crown, and Philip had the crown. Orders were still orders, after all.

"I want an immediate assault launched upon Isle Turtledove," Philip said. "See to it."

"Sir," General Evans began to explain. "The rain has not yet subsided. Our troops have had difficulty maneuvering-"

"General, if you don't have the ability to carry out my commands, step aside for someone who will!" Philip cut in.

Silence fell. General Evans was deeply offended. Slowly he rose from his seat. "Sir," he said. "If you doubt my competence after all my years of faithful service, I offer my sword, which I have only drawn in defen-"

"Fine," Philip said, cutting off what would have been a very moving speech. "You're relieved. Who's next in line?"

Completely thrown, Evans looked helplessly around. "Ah…"

"That would be me, your majesty," piped up the officer next to him, one Roberts. He liked Evans personally and was sorry to see the old man go, but he also didn't want to pass up a chance at the top job.

"I'm Eggleston Roberts," he said. "I'm the general's deputy."

"Well, now you're in command," Philip said. "You have the army. You heard my orders. Can you do it?"

Roberts saluted. "Yes, sir!"

"Good," Philip said. "Begin the attack immediately. You're dismissed."

Roberts saluted again. Philip, without acknowledging the gesture, turned and stalked from the council chamber. Roberts scuttled out after him. Slowly the other generals filed out, leaving a bewildered Evans alone.

Roberts was not the same personality as his predecessor. Where General Evans was careful and attentive to all matters, Roberts was flashy and audacious. When his king told him to attack, he attacked. That very night he gave the orders. "We strike now!" he said jubilantly to the other generals, gathered in council in his war tent at the army's headquarters outside the city. "Tonight! First the dragons and the griffins from above, and then the men across the channel to finish up! They'll never see us coming!"

"Sir?" one of his lieutenants said hesitantly. "But with the rain, at night, won't our dragons and griffins have trouble seeing each other-"

"They'll be fine," Roberts said brusquely. "King Philip has spoken. We attack!"

A dragon attack is impressive in many respects. What it is most certainly not is quiet. This is particularly true when the attack takes place at night in the middle of a pouring rainstorm. Dragons, for obvious reasons, hate getting wet. An irritable dragon is not a pleasant one, nor especially a quiet one.

Thus the first thing Sally knew of the impending assault was not the classic blast of dragon flame or the howling of wind created by dragon wings, but a lot of bellowing and roaring as a number of wet and angry dragons slammed into each other, being unable to see clearly in the pouring rain. Some of the dragons tried to flame, but missed in the rain and instead hit each other or the water down below. Geysers of steam billowed up around them, making things even worse.

The griffins were even more upset. Being partly big cats, they didn't like getting wet either, and the addition of large irritable dragons flying around them didn't help matters at all. Many of them tried to break off and fly back to the mainland, but found other griffins or dragons in their way. Fighting broke out in the skies, and within ten minutes the air wing of Philip's army had descended into chaos, amid gushers of steam and flying feathers.

That left the ground troops. They had already set out in longboats across the channel, nervously looking up at the tumultuous skies overhead and clinging to their helmets. The longboats came on in swift lines towards the island, rowed by sturdy infantrymen pulling hard at the oars. The water below them was choppy, more so because of the multitude of dragon and griffin wings tearing overhead, but the boats still bounced along across the waves, heading straight for Isle Turtledove. Rain and mist dashed in the soldiers' faces. Sally saw them coming and reluctantly drew her sword. She wondered if she could try smiting them with light again. The problem was that she wasn't completely sure how she had done that the first time. "Maybe if I turn my hand just so…" she said, tentatively gesturing towards the oncoming lines of boats.

She meant to produce a golden wave of light that would drive the soldiers back, preferably without much injury, but leaving them suitably chastened. What instead happened was that the water in the channel parted, as easily as a maid throwing open a pair of curtains to let the sunlight into a room.

Sally found herself looking with utmost astonishment at wet sand and mud, with equally astonished fish flopping around in the puddles left behind. On either side of the newly created pathway through the channel, the boats carrying the soldiers crashed and bumped into each other, thrown aside by the turbulent waves. Several of the boats capsized, dumping their occupants headlong into the water. The officers commanding the attack yelled and blew signal horns, trying to gather their men together and regroup, but it was plainly hopeless. The lines were all mixed up, every formation was out of kilter, and no one knew whether to stay in the boats and go forward or abandon the boats and risk the new path in the sea, despite the danger that Sally might slam it shut on them at any moment.

In the end, one panicked lieutenant lost his head and blew the call for retreat. This caught on, and soon every man was either swimming or rowing back the way he had come. In the skies, the surviving dragons and griffins heard the calls and did the same. The attack wave fell back to the shore, confused and upset, in utter failure. Sally waited until the waters were clear before closing her hand. The path through the channel closed with it, to her great relief. She had worried the thing was going to stay stubbornly open.

Roberts, on shore, was thunderstruck. He had not expected his attack to collapse so spectacularly. Now, as his men came streaming back in bedraggled columns, and his singed and soaked dragons and griffins thudded in for messy landings, his generals approached and asked what to do. "Assemble in the command tent," he said weakly. "I'll meet you there."

As they slogged away into the mud, Roberts pulled himself together, came to a sudden resolution, and headed quickly in the other direction. He wasn't actually headed for the command tent. Some generals would've done the honorable thing and tendered their sword in resignation, or even more dramatically threatened to throw themselves upon it. Roberts was more practical. He had no intention of taking the blame for this. This had to be the work of supernatural powers, wizards or something, and clearly wasn't his fault. He obviously couldn't go back and explain this to King Philip, though. Rumors already ran through the camp about what had happened on board the Paragon. They grew in the telling, but the point remained the same. Roberts was certain that if he went to Philip and admitted his failure, he wouldn't survive the encounter.

There was clearly only one thing to do. He went back to his private tent, pulled on his cloak, and walked calmly into the night. In all the disorder of the returning army, no one saw him go. Indeed no one in Loventry ever saw him again. He lived out his days quietly in a nondescript bakery in Seyna, serving up breakfast rolls to travelers.

The generals took about an hour to realize what had happened. Once they realized that Roberts had flown the coop, they broke into an argument about which one of them should take command. None of them really wanted to be stuck with the army, but clearly something had to be done.

They were into their second hour of arguing when the door of the command tent opened. The closest officer to the door tried to head off the visitor. "This is the command tent," he bellowed, "and we are not to be disturbed!"

"I can solve your problem," the man said casually, his face partly hidden in the shadow of his cloak. "You don't want to take over the army, because you're afraid you'll fail and Philip will kill you. Fine. I'll take it over. I'll lead it, and I'll kill Philip myself."

The generals one and all rose from their seats in alarm. "Who on earth-" one began.

The man threw back his cloak. "I am Evinrude. Lord of House Charming. Rightful King of Loventry. This army is mine by right. This *kingdom* is mine by right. Philip is a pretender to the throne and a betrayer of the country. The Houses who sent the men of this army, the lords to whose banners you are sworn, they know this. Why do you think Lord Ryan and Lady Caroline are locked away? Who do you think murdered Lady Eulalie? Who do you think really murdered Lady Amaryllis and took this kingdom into war against Lydwin, a kingdom that never meant us harm before? The only way to set things right is to overthrow Philip and return the kingdom to its rightful allegiance. Are you with me?"

The officer near the door had raised his sword. He paused for one moment. Then he lifted his blade in salute. One by one the others did the same. Evinrude smiled. Outside the tent, so did Leon.

The Ballad of Evinrude and Eulalie

107

10: The Investigations of Peter

Peter, wizard of the Order of the Rabbit, didn't learn about Rowena's death until he arrived on Kirtle Island. His magical mirror, with which he kept in contact with the other members of his order and the High Council, had developed a glitch of some sort. Every time he tried to use the mirror, it buzzed for a bit, shimmered and flashed in its glass, and then eventually gave up and dimmed out. Peter had tried tapping it with his wand, turning it off and on again, but nothing worked. He suspected he would have to take it by a magical glazier when he returned to Loventry.

When he stepped off the ship in the port of Kirtle Island, he worried he would see the dragon corpse still there in the harbor. Not only was it still there, it was beginning to smell. Peter noticed that the streets seemed a bit more orderly than he would have thought, and he assumed the local police force had finally managed to get itself back together again. What he did not expect was to be approached by a scowling man in an apron. "You Peter? Rabbit wizard?"

"Yes…" Peter said cautiously, laying a hand surreptitiously on his wand.

"I run the White Beetle Inn," the man said. "Got a room prepared for you. Also a message. Here." He pushed a letter into Peter's hands. "Already paid for. This way." He turned and started towards the inn. Peter prudently decided not to question the man just then, and waited until he was settled in his room before opening the letter.

What he read stunned him. Rowena had been murdered. Lady Caroline and Lord Ryan of House Brendan were suspected. The Rabbit High Council had attempted to make inquiries about when they might stand trial, but had heard nothing so far. Evidently Philip had more important matters on his mind, such as waging war on Isle Turtledove.

Peter expected that the Council would call him back to lead the investigation, perhaps question the suspected murderers. To his surprise, however, Egmond, who had written the letter himself, expressly desired him to continue. "For all we know," Egmond wrote, "Rowena's murder and this may be connected. There is something foul in all this. A good Rabbit wizard does not just go and get herself poisoned needlessly."

Peter wasn't so sure about that. From his experience, anyone could go and get themselves poisoned, no matter what order they were in. With a sigh, however, he set the letter aside and calmly set about his task.

It was rough going at first. A number of the relevant witnesses to what Rowena had done, such as the members of the Kirtle Island police force, were long since buried or reduced to ashes. Others simply didn't want to talk about it. The rebuilt police force, acting on Rowena's last orders, had clamped down pretty hard while they waited for someone else to come tell them what to do. Swords had been confiscated, curfews imposed, and streets patrolled vigorously, until the whole island seemed on a constant knife's edge of tension. Against this, no one wanted much to talk to a strange wizard fresh off a ship asking uncomfortable questions about the previous wizard to come off a ship.

Peter had almost given up when he returned to the White Beetle after a fruitless afternoon of wandering the island. He sat alone at a table and motioned for a drink. The barmaid brought it to him, and he drank it moodily, pondering his next move. As none readily presented itself, he finally sighed, rose, and started for his room. He paused and absent-mindedly tugged at his pocket, digging out several coins and spilling them onto the table for the barmaid. Then he began to walk away.

"Well," he heard her say as he left. "'He's a right gentleman. Not like that other wand-wielder."

Peter stopped, caught by a sudden idea. "Excuse me," he said, wheeling around. "What other wand-wielder?"

"Oh," the barmaid said, flushing red, "I didn't mean no offense-"

"It's all right," Peter said hastily. "I didn't intend to eavesdrop, I'm just looking into a few things. I'm Peter, I'm a Rabbit wizard, you see, but not like Rowena."

"I'm glad to see that," the barmaid said. "We didn't like her. Didn't much like the other one either."

"Who was the other one?" Peter asked.

"Weren't sure what order he was in at first," the barmaid said. "Thought maybe he was a Squirrel. Could've even been a Rabbit, meanin' no offense."

"None taken," Peter said.

"But then," she said, "I saw him. On the dock. I was on m' way home after my shift, and there he was, talkin' to a dragon, big as you please!"

"A dragon," Peter said. "The same one-"

"Yeh!" she said. "The same one! Anyway, the dragon's right there, and he's set a boat on fire, and next thing I know this wizard's yellin' about he's Mortimer, in the Polecat order, and he's Rowena's *father*, would y' believe, and then someone *else* shoots the dragon in the *eye*, and then the dragon falls in the water an', well, y' can imagine. Should've known he was. Y'can always tell with them types. It's the eyes," she said knowingly.

Peter nodded as if he knew exactly what she was talking about, although actually he had no idea. In his experience Polecat wizards tended to have the same eyes as everyone else. That was what made it worse.

He considered, trying to take it all in. "So, this wizard Mortimer said he was Rowena's father?"

"Yeh," the barmaid said solemnly, lowering her voice. "And then we didn't see him after that. Ever. Some says he was murdered. But there would've been a body then, wouldn't there? Never did see one. But we didn't see him alive again anyway. And then Rowena left with a ship and a crew, good mates too, and we didn't see *them* after that either."

"I see," Peter said. "You said there was someone else. The one who shot the dragon."

"Oh, yeh," she said. "Rumors been flyin' all over about him. No one knows who he was. Coulda been a wizard. Coulda been someone else. There was some mercenary that got murdered too, but they're always getting whacked, comes with the job, right? And we did see his body, you know how I know? Whoever it was killed him left the body right here in the common room, and you'll never guess who had to clean it up and bury the poor man out back. Us barmaids, that's who. Mostly me, 'coz Diana fainted."

"I'm sorry," Peter said sympathetically. "You know, the murder rate around here does seem to have ticked up suddenly."

"Tell me about it," she said. "I got kids, you know. This used to be a nice friendly island, like. Now there's dragons moulderin' in the harbor and bodies in the common room and everything."

"I promise," Peter said, "I intend to do something about this. I'm a Rabbit. It's what we do." He rose, thanked the barmaid, and left.

Outside, he had to take a moment to think what to do. He could report all this to the Council, but at the moment, he had precious little to report. Rowena had a Polecat father who had maybe been murdered, and someone else had been on Kirtle and had killed a dragon and a mercenary. He didn't know who that someone else was, and as for hard evidence, what he had so far was the word of a barmaid. Peter believed her, but he didn't know if the Rabbit High Council would, not to mention King Philip.

He needed more. Particularly, what he needed was a body. Fortunately, as the barmaid had pointed out, there was a very large one right out there in Kirtle Island harbor.

As has already been noted, dead dragons smell pretty bad. The closer Peter got to this one, the stronger the stench grew. The islanders had tried to move it from the harbor, but not only do dead dragons smell a lot, they weigh a lot too. Peter made a few discreet inquiries and learned that they had even tried burning the corpse to ashes but had quickly run into the obvious problem that dragons are, by necessity, invulnerable to fire. He therefore resolved that as soon as he had finished with his investigation, he would magically relieve them of their burden and restore the harbor to its natural cleanliness.

It didn't take Peter long to find the late Mortimer's mark on the dragon. He recognized it at once. It was a standard Polecat death curse, guaranteed to slay instantly any living creature it touched. Peter conjured a sturdy knapsack, and with a bit of very careful wandwork managed to sever the bit of dragonskin that had the mark on it from the rest of the dragon, before finally transferring the skin into the knapsack. It took him at least an hour and a half to do this, and it was tricky work, but at the end of it, he had his proof: undeniable, to those who could understand, that Mortimer the wizard was a Polecat.

He looked over the dragon once more, just to make sure he hadn't missed anything, and noticed the remains of the arrow in what was left of the dragon's eye. The magical traces weren't quite as clear as they had once been, but Peter was still able to work them out. To his surprise, they led into the Kirtle Island village. They also had the distinct greyish air of death about them, which meant that whoever had loosed the arrow at the dragon was now dead himself. "Hm," Peter mused. "I wonder…" He retrieved the arrow, and stowed that in his knapsack as well, then carefully conjured a clean-up spell that vaporized the dragon corpse and wafted away the remaining smells. There was a smattering of applause from a few passing islanders heading home before nightfall. Peter acknowledged the applause with a slightly bemused wave, before hurrying to follow the traces from the arrow.

It didn't take him long to find the mercenary's body. As the barmaid had said, it was buried behind the White Beetle, in a small cleared out patch of ground. From what Peter guessed, it seemed the innkeeper had set aside that patch of ground particularly for customers who met untimely ends at his establishment. The graves were unmarked, but for Peter, the magical traces were unmistakable. He quickly found the place where the mercenary lay. Unfortunately, the magic ended there. The best Peter could do without unearthing the body was to determine that the man had been killed by a non-magical weapon, probably an ordinary sword. He decided to let the mercenary lie in peace.

The Rabbit wizard sighed as he walked away. It would've been so much easier if the mercenary had been murdered by something magical. Now Peter was going to have to do this the hard way. The only sure way to unravel the mystery of why the mercenary and Rowena's father, not to mention Rowena, had been murdered was to track the mercenary back to his employer. That meant Peter was going to have to go to Ilariana.

The next question was how. It was too late that evening to book passage on a ship. Peter could wait until the next day and make discreet inquiries about ships heading to Miralycia, the port which would set him on the road to the inland city of Ilariana, headquarters of the Mercenary Guild. On the other hand, who knew what might happen while he was stuck on the ship? He couldn't afford to waste more time. Reluctantly, Peter went downstairs to the innkeeper, who was just closing up the bar, and explained that he was leaving.

"Already?" the man said in surprise. "Don't you need a place to sleep?"

"Ah, no," Peter said. "Change of plans."

The man politely asked no questions. The bill was settled up, and soon Peter and his knapsack of belongings, including the dragon-skin, were outside the White Beetle Inn, alone in the dark.

He took firm hold on his wand, pictured Ilariana on a map in his mind, and reached into his pocket. His spare sock was there as always. Peter clutched his sock in one hand and his wand in the other, fixed his destination firmly in mind, and said the proper words. Kirtle Island spun away behind him into a whirl of argyle and fuzz, white and dark, a blur of socks of all kinds. Then the socks parted, and the blur resolved into proper form once again. The next moment, he landed face-first in a massive sand dune. He emerged, spluttering, to find himself face to face with a startled jackal. The jackal quickly readied itself to spring, evidently quite pleased with dinner suddenly landing conveniently in front of it.

Peter, unlike other wizards of his order, wasn't keen on animals, particularly not animals that wanted to eat him. He drew his wand and sent up a flare of blazing light into the night sky. The jackal yipped in alarm and hurried away. Peter struggled out of the sand dune, pocketed his sock, and hurried in the opposite direction. This was a corollary to the most important rule of magical transportation; not only do you need to keep your destination firmly in mind, you need to be very precise about it. Otherwise, instead of landing nicely in the city, you wind up face-first in a sand dune.

Fortunately, having arrived near the city, he didn't have to go far. Peter ran past a few more sand dunes and around a clump of palm trees, until suddenly the white towers and curving walls of Ilariana rose in the moonlight before him. He could also see the gates of the city, which were unfortunately closed at that late hour. Ilariana was famously hospitable to travelers, but only up to a point. The desert, after all, turned deadly at night.

Peter sighed, conjured up a tent, and settled in by the palm trees. .He would venture into the city in the morning. One way or another, no matter how long it took, he would sort out who had murdered Rowena, her father, and the mercenary. Whoever they were, they would be brought to justice. That was what Rabbit wizards did.

11: Paradise

Constance and Gilbert, meanwhile, had just cleared Level Six of Purgatory. They had flown past miles of lush and verdant trees laden with fruit that the penitent souls could never reach, although Constance had snatched an apple from one tree as she passed.

"You're not really supposed to do that, you know!" Gilbert said, as leaves fluttered down around him in their wake.

"Why not?" Constance replied as they closed in the stairway for Level Six. "They come in handier than you'd think!"

The two angels, still with Amaryllis in tow, charged up the stairway, burst out, and paused, finding themselves confronted by an immense wall of fire. The flames rose as high as they could see, crackling and roaring in a tumult of everlasting fury. Constance hesitated; she knew she was an angel and therefore invulnerable, but even so one never knew about blazing walls of fire in Purgatory.

Just then, a soul dashed past her and plunged headlong into the fire, yelling out "Woohoo, chastity!" as it did so. Constance's mouth dropped open. "What the-"

"That," said Gilbert quickly, to forestall what he was sure would be a breach of angelic policy, "would be Level Seven. In this level, souls are purged from, ah, vices of an improper sexual nature." He twitched just slightly, wishing Constance hadn't blown up his wing sanitizer. Gilbert had been dreading this terrace for hours.

"Oh," Constance said. "Well, then, we shouldn't have a problem. We're both angels, yeah? And I ditched my ex-boyfriend Ben ages ago. He was the Antichrist, long story. So we're cool!"

"We should be," Gilbert said. "Unless..." He turned doubtfully back, and looked back at Amaryllis. "You weren't...ah... involved with that Evinrude gentleman, were you? No, ah, impure thoughts?"

"No!" Amaryllis said furiously. "Not in the least. Not one *bit!*"

"Excellent!" Gilbert sighed, deeply relieved. "Right, then, here we go." He took hold of Amaryllis's arm, and started for the wall of fire.

Constance had caught a slight note in Amaryllis's voice, something that set her intuition going. "Hey, Gilbert, I'm not sure that's such a good idea-"

But it was too late. They had jumped in. There was a terrific thunderclap, the fire cracked and snapped, and Amaryllis was thrown back violently into the terrace, taking Gilbert with her.

"You lied!" Gilbert protested as he clambered to his feet.

"No, I didn't!' Amaryllis said defensively. "You asked if I'd had impure thoughts about Evinrude. I didn't, I swear it. Even though I was betrothed to him, I had not one impure thought about that man."

Constance arched an eyebrow. "Okay, did you have impure thoughts about anyone *else?*"

Amaryllis blushed, turning her ghostly form a distinct shade of rose. "Well…maybe. There was Philip."

"Philip? The guy who… he *murdered you!*" Constance said, horrified.

"Well, yes. I knew that the moment his people shot me with an arrow. I wouldn't want to marry him, of course. But he did talk politics with me. That's important! He respected my mind!" Amaryllis said. She gave a dreamy sigh. "We spent all night talking about politics…."

"But…" Constance said again. "But he *murdered* you!"

"Well," Amaryllis said, thoughtfully, "In the broader scheme of things it was justifiable. I know what Philip's policies would've been if he became king, because he told me. Evinrude never told me anything. You know what we talked about? The weather. If he'd cared to have any more conversations with me instead of running off after *her*, we might have moved on to sporting events. Maybe, just maybe, he would've given me a real treat and we would've talked about falcon hunts!" she spat out. "I don't think Evinrude ever had a real policy idea in his life, and if he did, he wouldn't have cared enough to share it with me. The idea that man could be king of Loventry!"

"But…" Constance said for the third time, hoping that maybe her point would get across, "he *murdered* you!"

"It was for a good cause! He wouldn't have become king otherwise!" Amaryllis said. "Even if it did hurt, and he should've told me, and I honestly wouldn't have thought-" her voice broke.

Gilbert stepped in, slightly hesitant. "It did hurt, didn't it, when you died? I have some little experience in this area, you see." He gestured towards her side. "Arrow, wasn't it?""

"Yes," Amaryllis said tightly. "It was."

"I'm so sorry," Gilbert said, and he meant it. He always meant it. Gilbert had, for the moment, forgotten the mission. He was on duty again.

"I never had the chance to say goodbye," Amaryllis said, "To anyone. Not that there was much of anyone to say goodbye to. I didn't have much family. That's why I got matched up with Evinrude so easily, you see; my immediate parents have passed on, and my relatives, House Marian?" her voice caught again. "Well, they needed someone expendable. So did Evinrude's parents. It was all politics. I made a good alliance. So I know, I'll go back to Loventry, marry Evinrude, and set things right. The kingdom will be safe from Philip. That's all that matters."

Silently, the sunglasses covering her eyes slid away and vanished. Amaryllis looked down at the ground. There was a long pause. Then Constance's fist clenched, and light flashed around her. "No," she said, eyes blazing. "No, it darn well isn't."

"Language- oh, never mind," Gilbert said.

"You're not going to go back and marry Evinrude," Constance said. "We'll get it fixed some other way."

"Really?" Amaryllis said, still a little doubtfully.

"Yeah," Constance said. "I'm not doing it. I'm not having you stuck up with some guy like my ex-boyfriend Ben or some other guy who shoots you with an arrow. Not happening."

"But what can we do?" Amaryllis said. "We're trapped here, aren't we?"

"Question," Constance said. "Do you have any impure thoughts about Philip now? Like, right now?"

"No," Amaryllis said, her voice still a little quavery. "Not right now."

"Good," Constance said. "By the angelic power vested in me, I declare you absolved of the vices of impurity, envy, and all incidents and attendants therewith. In nomine Patris, et Filis, et Spiritus Sancti, etcetera. Now, go long!"

With that, before Gilbert or Amaryllis realized what was happening, Constance had snatched Amaryllis up and hurled her right into the wall of fire. Gilbert flinched, expecting another bang. Instead, Amaryllis disappeared. The fire crackled behind her. In the distance, they heard a muffled *thud*.

"It worked!" Constance said happily as she ran forward into the fire. "I'm a genius!"

"We're not out yet!" Gilbert said, right behind her. "There's one more part of Purgatory we have to go through!"

"But that's the last level, wasn't it?" Constance said, just as the fire around them came to an end. "There can't possibly be anything left...." Her voice trailed off into wonder. They had come, quite abruptly, into a magnificent garden.

The fire died away behind them. Around them rose a forest of mighty trees, brilliant in green and yellow leaves, many with fruits of unknown kinds glimmering beneath their branches. Constance had never before seen such beautiful trees, so tall that they blocked out the sky overhead, so bright that even her own halo seemed dim by comparison. She couldn't think of anything to say to express her amazement. Even Gilbert, who had some idea of what was coming, had fallen silent. It was one thing to know in theory; it was quite another thing to find oneself faced with reality.

Amaryllis had been lying just beside them on the ground where she had landed; now she rose. "Thanks for that," she said. "Good thing it worked."

"Yeah, yeah," Constance said, recovering herself. "What is this place?"

"The Earthly Paradise," Gilbert said. "Also known as the Garden of-"

"Eden?" Constance cut in. "Wait a minute. I thought that place was guarded. By a great big angel with a flaming sword or something."

"I shouldn't think so, not anymore," Gilbert assured her. "After all, to even get here one would have to go through all of Purgatory and pass through that wall of fire, and besides, that was most likely a literary flourish."

"*Oh no,*" said a new voice, "*It's real. Guess how I know.*"

"Boris," Constance groaned, "Not you."

"*Me,*" said the angel, stepping out from behind a tree and raising a gigantic sword, which this time didn't just glow but was definitely on fire. "*I was reassigned. It was felt that guarding the gates of Purgatory was beyond my capabilities if I could be so easily overwhelmed by a bottle of wing sanitizer. So I was given lighter duties. After untold millennia of never failing in my watch, I was given lighter duties!*" Boris fairly blazed with umbrage.

"You could look at it like a vacation?" Constance offered.

"*I am an angel! Guardian of the gates!*" Boris thundered, and the very ground shook beneath their feet. "*I do not require a vacation!*"

Constance was considering throwing her apple at Boris and making it explode when suddenly Gilbert raised a hand. "You know," he said, "That sounds somewhat prideful."

"*What?*" said Boris in booming tones that shook the leaves from the trees.

"One might say," Gilbert said casually, "That an angel should be grateful to be wherever he is posted. As it says in the Scriptures, are we not all ministering spirits sent to serve?"

"*What?*" Boris said again, in slightly less booming tones. The angel obviously hadn't considered things from this point of view.

"Does it really say that?" Constance whispered.

"Of course it does," Gilbert said. "Hebrews, chapter one, verse fourteen. Didn't you take the Scriptural references course when you became an angel?"

"Er, no," Constance said, "I must have missed that one."

"I should take the remedial course when I get back, were I you," Gilbert said kindly. "A thorough knowledge of the Scriptures is essential in our line of work."

"I'll get right on that," Constance said. "I'm sure I can talk to someone-"

"*Excuse me,*" Boris interrupted. "*If we could get back to the main point here?*"

"Oh, yes, yes, of course," Gilbert said. There followed a slightly embarrassed pause. "What was the point?"

"We were trying to get to Heaven," Constance said. "Before Eulalie does. Remember?"

"Right, yes," Gilbert said. He checked his clipboard. "There's still time. But only just. She seems to be just outside the gates."

"Great," Constance said. "Well, it's been nice talking to you, Boris, old pal, but we've got to go now. Bye!" She started to fly past him.

"*Wait,*" Boris said, still confused. "*I did not say you could enter this garden.*"

"But we're already in it," Constance said reasonably, "And now we're leaving again, okay? Okay, cool. Bye again!"

"*What?*" Boris said.

"Farewell!" Gilbert said. "Read up on your Scriptures, there's a good guardian. I can recommend a course!" Then he quickly flew after Constance, making sure that Amaryllis was safely in tow. Boris, mightily bewildered, was left in their wake amidst the trees.

Constance waited until they were safely out of earshot before she burst into laughter. "Oh, that was *brilliant!*" she cackled. "*Brilliant!*"

"Yes, I thought so," Gilbert said, smiling for once. "But you did well at the end too. I wonder where he'll be assigned next?"

"Hopefully nowhere near me," Constance said. "Okay. So, what now? How do we get from here to-"

Before she could even say the word, they had, without realizing it, reached the exact center of the Garden. At that moment, the two angels and Amaryllis were suddenly surrounded by a column of blinding light. The Garden, Purgatory, and all of Earth around it disappeared below them, as all of space fell away into the glow.

Golden clouds gathered around them. For the first time in a while, both Constance and Gilbert breathed a little freer and their wings stretched. Then the light fell away. Before them at last rose the Pearly Gates.

To Constance's great surprise, there was a line. Heaven was, she had learned, a little more orderly than that. "Eulalie's probably in there somewhere," she said, scanning the line quickly. Then she realized she had a problem. "I don't know what she looks like!"

"I might be able to look it up," Gilbert said. He tapped his clipboard. A sketch materialized in black and white. Gilbert tapped again, and color neatly blossomed out amidst the lines. "Ah," he said, "She's blond. A bit willowy. And tall."

Constance looked at the sketch, and then shot a glance over the line again. "I think I see her!" she said joyfully. Then she looked farther. "Wait, no, that's her! No..." Constance sighed. "Can you narrow it down a bit?"

"I can try," Gilbert said. "But-"

"Actually, I have a better idea," Constance said. She stepped forward, raised her hand, and whistled, giving it an angelic twist. The supernaturally magnified whistle shrieked piercingly down the length of the Pearly Gates.

"Hey!" Constance yelled, as everyone in the line turned to look at her. "I need your attention! I'm looking for Lady Eulalie of House Turtledove, kingdom of Loventry. Eulalie, if you're in this line, I need to talk to you, like now!" There was a slight buzz, as the human souls in the line looked around to see if one of them might be the sought-after Eulalie. Then in the distance, Constance saw one of the souls leave its place and come forward. To her relief, the soul matched Gilbert's description.

"Hello," she said as she approached Constance, "I'm Lady Eulalie. Is this about when we can get into Heaven? I've been waiting for a while, you see."

"Not exactly," Constance said truthfully. She wondered how she was going to explain what she was there to do. Then the situation changed dramatically when Amaryllis saw Eulalie.

"You," Amaryllis said, "You stole Evinrude from me. I've decided I'm not going to marry him anymore, so you're welcome to him, but even so. You should apologize."

"What?" Eulalie said, confused. "I'm dead, aren't I? I can't marry anyone now I'm dead. And I'm not even sure I know you, and what do you mean I stole Evinrude, I never, we've only been writing-"

"I read what you were writing, you sounded awfully friendly-"

"Because we *were* friends, we were never more than that, and what do you mean you read what I-"

Constance whistled again, forgetting that she had turned up the power on her whistle. Everyone within a mile clapped their hands to their ears. "Sorry!" Constance called. "My fault!" Then she turned back to Eulalie and Amaryllis. "Okay, look. Let me cut to the chase.

Loventry's in trouble. Philip's taken over, and he's a jerk. Your guy, whoever's guy, I lost track, Evinrude is on a vengeance thing, and he needs to be stopped. My original plan was to bring both of you back to Loventry and have Amaryllis marry Evinrude like you were going to, sort everything out that way. But now I'm not sure that's the right way to go. So here's the deal. Do either of you really want to go back?"

Amaryllis and Eulalie looked at each other. Then Eulalie squared her shoulders. "I do. I got flamed by a dragon and never even had the chance to find out why. I'd like to save my island at least, and the rest of the country as well."

Amaryllis started to say something, but looked towards the Pearly Gates. The look was enough. Constance nodded. "Okay. New plan." She looked at Eulalie. "You wait here. Gilbert, stay with her. Amaryllis, follow me." Then, Constance marched towards the Pearly Gates.

At the very head of the line, two angels were fussing around an intercom set into the wall. "We need to call Zechariah," one of them was saying as Constance approached. "He's always been good with these things, he'll know!"

"He's on duty!" the other angel said in distress.

"What's going on?" Constance asked.

"The intercom shorted," the first angel explained. "So we can't check each person in through Records from here, which means we have to do it all by word of mouth. Which is why there's a delay."

Constance looked at the intercom. "You try giving it a good swift kick?" she suggested helpfully.

"No!" the angel said, horrified. "This is Heaven! We would not kick it! Not in Heaven! We talk to it. Gently. We acknowledge its feelings. We make it feel like it's wanted, like it's loved."

Constance arched an eyebrow. "Oh. Well, have you tried that?"

"Yes," the angel said. "It's not working."

"Let me try," Constance said. She approached the intercom, bent down, and whispered very sweetly, "Hello. I'm Constance. If you don't start working by the time I count to three, I'm going to send you straight down to the Bad Place. You don't want to know what they do to intercoms down there. You really, *really* don't. I'd rather keep you up here, but they only let functional working intercoms stay up here. Your choice. So. One."

Nothing happened.

"*Two.*"

In an instant sweet strains of harp music poured from the intercom and the Pearly Gates swung open. Cheering rose from the line of souls.

"How did you do that?" the angel gasped.

Constance smiled. "I made it feel loved."

As the line of souls resumed its orderly procession into the gates of Heaven, accompanied by the distant strains of golden harp music and the harmonizing of the Angel Choir, Constance turned to Amaryllis. "Well," she said, "In you go, then. I'd say good luck, but it's Heaven. You don't really need it."

"But..." said Amaryllis.

"Go!" said Constance, giving her a push. "You've got family in there, right? Go say hi!"

Amaryllis started. Then she paused, and looked at Eulalie. "I'm sorry about Evinrude. I hope you're happy with him if he turns back to good. I really do."

Eulalie wasn't sure if Amaryllis was entirely sincere, but she would never know. Amaryllis stepped forward, joined the line, and within moments had passed the Pearly Gates and vanished into the clouds beyond. Constance sighed. "Another one bites the dust," she said happily.

"What?" Gilbert said.

"It's an Earth song. You wouldn't get it. Anyway, back to Loventry!" She extended her wings and snapped her fingers, and she, Eulalie, and Gilbert vanished from the Pearly Gates in a flash of light.

12: Confrontation

Philip had left orders that he was not to be disturbed once he had withdrawn into the castle that night except in an emergency or unless Isle Turtledove had fallen. He had enough confidence in the sheer power of his army that he was not about to stay up and wait for news of an attack he was certain would be successful. Thus Philip had gone to sleep while his soldiers marched to war.

He was therefore greatly surprised to be shaken awake out of a sound sleep by an absolutely terrified officer. "What the devil-" he began. He couldn't remember the man's name. Judging by the man's uniform colors, Philip assumed that he was one of the original knights sworn to House Shirley's banner before Philip had assumed the throne and assembled Loventry's army.

"Sir," the officer said in a low, rapid voice, "I'm sorry, you've got to come with me now. Right this minute."

"Captain," Philip said, making a guess as to the man's rank, "You forget yourself. I am the king of-"

"There's no time!" the man said desperately. "You'll be dead in a minute! The whole army's turned on you! We've got to run *now!*" Before Philip could protest or even fully grasp what was happening, the officer grabbed him by the arm and heaved him bodily towards the door.

He hurried Philip out of the castle and into the night, ignoring the king's splutters of outrage. Philip was on the point of turning around and marching right back inside, intent on demanding the officer's resignation or his head, he didn't particularly care which. Then he happened to look out, away from the castle, and see the tents of the army spread out before him, with the castle of Isle Turtledove visible off in the distance.

Philip was standing on a low rise overlooking the field where his tents were gathered neatly around his royal banners. Rather, they were gathered where his banners should have been. Now knots of men were busily pulling them down. Philip could see brief scuffles breaking out in some places as a few loyalists tried to protect his flags, but they were quickly and neatly overpowered. It was only then that he heard a rumbling in the distance, a rumbling punctuated by the staccato thuds of heavy armored feet.

"That'll be the dragons coming," the officer behind him said. "I told you, the army, the knights, they've all turned. They don't want you anymore."

"But why?" Philip said. He couldn't fathom it. Had Roberts' attack on the island failed?

"Turns out," the officer said, and suddenly his voice had changed, "They wanted someone else instead."

Philip turned. The officer looked different now. He had drawn aside the cloak he'd been wearing. "Cloak of disguise," the man said, letting it fall indifferently to the ground. "Took it off one of your former associates. Comes in useful."

"Who are you?" Philip said.

The man laughed, just a little. "Figures you wouldn't know. You never even met me. You had your Prime Minister kill me. No, I forget, you had your Prime Minister arrange my death by sending me off to my death on a faraway island. Couldn't even do it yourselves. You may notice I have a little more courtesy than that."

"Evinrude," Philip said. "Of course. You're back. Should've known Rowena couldn't have done her job right."

"Oh, she succeeded," Evinrude said, drawing his sword. "I just didn't stay dead. I don't expect you'll have the same problem."

"You won't," Leon chimed in, emerging from behind a tree. "I called in a favor with the boss. Where you're going, you're gonna stay there."

"Who're you?" Philip said.

"Leon. I work with him," Leon said, tossing a wave at Evinrude. "Oh, and just so you know, he's got control of the army now."

"Is that right?" Philip said.

"It is," Evinrude said. "The army of Loventry has returned to its rightful allegiance."

Philip drew his own sword. "Well then, I suppose you have some sort of melodramatic speech to give me before you attack? How I murdered your lady love, vengeance is yours at last, and so on?"

Evinrude didn't even flinch. "No. Leon?"

Red fire blasted from Leon's hands. Philip's screams echoed for a few blinding seconds in the woods. Then he was gone. "Scuse me," Leon said. "I'm gonna need to escort his soul down now. Back in a bit."

Before he could leave, however, he was interrupted by a sudden bang and a flash of light. "All right!" Constance said as she materialized, Gilbert and Eulalie appearing right behind her. "Here we come to save the day!"

She skidded into silence the moment she looked around and saw Leon, Evinrude, and the little heap of ash wafting around on the ground. The smell of smoke still lingered in the air. Worse, Constance and Gilbert could see what Eulalie could not: the desolate soul of Philip, waiting to be taken down to Hell.

"Leon," Constance said slowly, in the same tone as a mother who has just found her toddler writing in crayon upon the walls, "What did you just do?"

"He made me!" Leon whined, pointing to Evinrude.

"Seriously?" Constance said. "The human made you do it?"

"We had a deal!" Leon said. "I help him get vengeance, I get his soul in the end. Well, he's got his vengeance now, yeah? A deal's a deal!" He turned to Evinrude. "I'll take you both down to-"

"No!" Eulalie said, throwing herself between Evinrude and Leon. "Take me instead!"

"Oh, for heaven's sake," Constance said, grabbing Eulalie by the arm and pulling her back.

"Language!" Gilbert said, unable to resist.

"Now?" Constance said, glaring. "You want to do this now? That wasn't even a bad word!"

"Now hang on-" Leon started to object.

"You can't-" Evinrude began.

"Actually," Gilbert said.

"Let me go!" Eulalie protested.

"Everybody *shut up!*" Constance snapped, so loudly that everyone actually did. Even the dragons in the distance paused.

"Okay," Constance said. "One at a time. Evinrude, did you tell Leon to do … that?" She gestured towards the ash still wafting desolately on the ground.

"Of course he did," Philip said, forgetting for a moment that since he was dead, no one living could hear him.

Constance held up her hand. "I was talking to Evinrude," she said.

Gilbert understood perfectly what was going on, of course, but Evinrude looked confused. "I'm sorry," he said, "But who are you? And is there someone else with you?"

"Honestly," Constance said, rolling her eyes hard, "This is getting out of hand. Gil, can I just resurrect him? It'd make things so much easier."

Gilbert sighed. "All right. You might as well."

Constance snapped her fingers. The ash whipped itself together into human form, and with a jerk, Philip's soul snapped back into it. "Ow!" Philip exclaimed the moment his body finished knitting itself back together.

"You shut up, again," Constance said.

Evinrude, meanwhile, was thoroughly shocked. "What magic is this?"

"I'm an angel, duh," Constance said. "I'm on the other side of your guy."

"Fine," Leon snapped. "Then we'll do this *again!*" With that, he unleashed a new blast of red fire. Philip disintegrated into ash.

"Now wait just a moment-" a horrified Gilbert started to say.

"*That* does it," Constance said, and snapped her fingers a second time. With a loud pop, ash and soul whipped back together. Philip was alive again. "Now," she said, drawing her golden sword, "Are we going to stand here and keep disintegrating and resurrecting this idiot all night long or what?"

Leon drew his own sword; the blade smoked and burned with a dark red light. "Fine," he said, "Let's fight."

Suddenly the trees behind him crunched into a flurry of leaves and shattered timbers. Several large dragons had just emerged onto the field, they and their riders evidently curious as to what was going on.

"Oh, good," Constance said, "What we really need now is *more* people."

"This will be my new army," Evinrude said. "Now, whoever all of you are, what I want to know is, are you with Philip or-"

"Actually," Leon said, "It's *my* new army."

"Actually," said the man riding the lead dragon, leaping down from the monster's back and striding up to the group, "It's mine."

He was tall and thin, and very sharp-elbowed, and for the occasion he had donned a long black cloak. Constance gasped. "Wait, I know you, you're-"

"Asmodeus," he said wheezily, "Arch-demon. I've been sending reinforcements, since Leon here seems to have bungled this job so badly."

"It's not my fault," Leon whined. "She keeps getting in the way!"

"Do you remember what happened to Ben?" Asmodeus said casually. "It's an unpleasant story, for some anyway. They still haven't found his spleen. But don't worry, there's plenty of other internal organs to torture. I've heard the small intestine is coming into favor these days."

Leon winced and fell silent. "Now then," Asmodeus began, "As for the rest of you…"

Like many of the others there that night, he was interrupted. Sally chose that unfortunate moment to arrive on scene. She had heard Constance's distant shout from the shores of Isle Turtledove, recognized the voice, and had assumed things were on the move. She had first taken a moment to make sure everyone on the island was secure. Then she had drawn her sword, grabbed her halo, and willed herself to transport to wherever Constance was. The problem was that she hadn't accounted for everyone else being there. As a result, when she arrived, she slammed right into Asmodeus, sending him ricocheting into his own dragon like one pool ball hitting another.

The dragon, being large and stupid, didn't realize who had just slammed into it, and flamed instinctively. Unfortunately for it, demons are by nature inflammable. Asmodeus wasn't injured in the blast, but for the first time in many long millennia of evildoing he lost his usually carefully controlled temper. The arch-demon leapt to his feet and slew the dragon with a burst of dark-magic death curses. In his fury, however, he forgot to disintegrate it, whereupon the massive corpse of the slain dragon toppled right over on him. There was a definite muffled *crunch*.

"Well, then," Constance said. "Now what?"

"Perhaps," Gilbert said carefully, "We should all get out of here before he extricates himself."

"Good plan," Constance said.

"Wait!" Evinrude said. "The men. The army. I will not leave them! And who are all of you anyway?"

"Oh, there's also Isle Turtledove," Sally said, "I don't want that guy attacking it, whoever he is."

"And who are you?" Evinrude demanded.

"Your guardian angel," Sally said, with a sigh. "Hello. My name's Sally. We're going to need to talk."

"My what?" Evinrude said.

"Guardian angel," Constance said. "They're supposed to keep charge over you, serve and protect, watch over your soul, and so on. At least I think they are, I'm not in the Guardian Corps. I'm sort of on special assignment these days."

"Serve and protect?" Evinrude said bitterly. "Then where was she when Eulalie got flamed?"

"That is an excellent question," Lady Eulalie said. "I was alone on that beach, as I recall. I do not remember an angel ever being there. Father Thomas can tell you, I attended Mass quite religiously. I expect he'll be at evening prayers now; you can ask him!"

"Ah," Sally said. "About that...."

Constance almost said a very bad word, but she just managed to restrain herself. "You forgot to mention you lost him too!"

"They stabbed him with a sword!" Sally wailed. "It happened too fast!"

"They killed Father Thomas?" Eulalie said in shock.

"Gilbert?" Constance said, looking at the angel. "Is there any chance...?"

"No," Gilbert said, looking over his clipboard after giving it a quick tap. "He's already in Heaven."

Constance shrugged. "Right, okay. Sorry, Eulalie, I didn't know. She left that part out when she filled me in."

"Well..." Eulalie said shakily, "The point is... what was the point?"

"The point," Evinrude said, "is that you angels don't seem to be doing a very good job protecting us. And you're surprised I turned to him?"

"Told ya," Leon said. "Anyhow, a deal is still a deal. You got the army, you killed your guy, I get your soul."

"But he's not dead yet," Evinrude said. "He – where is he?"

It was only then that they realized Philip wasn't there anymore. In the confusion with Asmodeus and the dragon, Philip had shrewdly seized the moment to make a run for it and dashed away into the woods.

Evinrude said a word so foul it shocked even Constance. Then he grabbed Leon by the scruff of his neck. "Find him," he snarled, "Or our deal's off."

"All right, all right!" Leon whimpered, surprised by the man's ferocity. "I'll find the guy, okay? I'll find him!" Then he disappeared in smoke.

"Now hold on-" Constance began.

"No," Evinrude said. "You lost him. You failed to protect her," he gestured towards Eulalie. "I don't really see why I need you." Then he turned on his boot heel and ran off into the woods on his own search for Philip.

The angels and Eulalie stood alone. Sally struggled to hold back her sobs. "I didn't expect it to go this badly," she hiccupped. "I tried!"

Constance sighed. "It doesn't always go well in this business. I lost a whole planet full of people once. I got a few of them back, though. Long story."

A silence fell in the woods. "So…" Gilbert said. "What shall we do now? I suppose I should go back to Earth and resume the duty."

"No," Constance said, "We haven't finished here yet. We need to set things right."

"How?" Sally said, wiping her nose with an angel feather she plucked from her wing.

"There is always a way," Constance said grimly. "Always."

She might have said something else inspiring, but it was her turn to be interrupted again, for at that moment the ground cracked with a sudden boom as Asmodeus exploded out from under the slain dragon. "Not anymore!" he roared in a blaze of anger. Then he charged straight at them.

Constance planted her feet. Frantic ideas flashed through her mind of smiting the arch-demon with a plague of hail or a wave of light, or perhaps simply hitting him with her angelic sword. She snapped her fingers, hoping something dramatic and judgmental would materialize and drive Asmodeus away.

What appeared was a bear, specifically, a very cross mama grizzly bear. Asmodeus scoffed. "A bear. Really."

"Oh yeah," Constance said. "I've got history with this bear, see. She and I had a tangle a little while back over some cubs I got in between by mistake. I just recognized her. Ooh, she does *not* look happy at all."

She wasn't wrong. The mama grizzly bear had, in fact, just been on the brink of settling down for a long winter's nap with her cubs and was none too happy to be pulled away. She looked around, saw Asmodeus, and came to the swift conclusion that he had played this trick upon her. The mama grizzly bear immediately swiped a massive paw at the arch-demon, bowling him over. Asmodeus bounded to his feet, spitting fire, but he had been distracted for a vital moment, and that was all Constance needed. "Begone!" she yelled, drawing her sword. "Get thee hence! In the name of the Father and the Son and the Holy Spirit, *shoo!*"

Light flooded the woods, so brilliant that it snapped away the shadows in the woods like rubber bands. Asmodeus vanished, howling. Leon chose that inopportune moment to reappear, dragging Philip by the scruff of his neck. "Found him!" Leon said excitedly. Then he yelped as the light blasted into him. The demon promptly vanished away again, leaving Philip behind. There was a distant roaring as a number of the dragons howled and burned away; many of them had been smuggled in by Asmodeus and Leon, and when they went, the dragons went. Within a few moments, Philip's army was substantially diminished.

Constance slid her sword back into its sheath, and the light dimmed. The mama grizzly bear looked around in abject puzzlement. Constance reached out a tentative hand. "All right, now," she said, "Back to Earth you go, that's right, there's a good bear." She patted the mama bear's muzzle gingerly then snapped, and the bear disappeared. The mama bear materialized shortly thereafter on Earth, where she would live a long and peaceful life with her cubs, having forgotten all about the great adventure in which she had briefly participated.

That left the three angels and Lady Eulalie alone, facing Philip. The erstwhile king of Loventry rose to his feet. "Well now," he said, "Evinrude seems to have gone away. That's all right. I don't know how he's alive, but I'll kill him again, you'll see. You'll just see!"

"With what army?" Constance said.

A tree collapsed into ashes behind her. Philip smiled. "You've forgotten? If Evinrude's run off, and you've driven away whoever those people were, I can seize back the remaining dragons and the rest of the army. They'll return to their rightful allegiance. All I have to do is rally them. I know their ways, you see, I've picked up a few dark wizard tricks here and there, working with Alistair and the rest."

From his belt he produced a horn made of dark twisted metal. "All I have to do is blow this, and every dragon still left in the country will come to my aid. The griffins and the others will follow. This ends now."

He raised the horn, but he never got the chance to blow it. Constance flung her halo like a golden Frisbee and dashed it from his hand, whereupon it exploded in a blaze of light. More dragons wandered away, and Philip's army grew still smaller.

"You were saying?" Constance said sweetly.

"Ah…" said Philip, speechless for once.

Then Evinrude emerged from behind the shattered tree that had been behind Constance. "Not much of a last word, is it? I would've expected more from you. At least an 'I surrender', as a courtesy." He strode to where Philip stood, and leveled his blade at the man. "On your knees," he snarled. "Now."

Philip raised his own blade. They scuffled briefly, but the outcome was obvious to anyone knowledgeable enough in swordsmanship to follow. Evinrude hadn't paid much attention to politics and the administrative details of running a kingdom during his schooling, but he was very good with his sword. Philip, by contrast, was an excellent schemer and a master at politics, but he was absolutely lousy at the martial arts. He tried an opening flurry of blows in a vague attempt at something he thought was called the Falk Fusillade, but in fact was nothing of the kind. Evinrude parried that easily. Philip tried several more things, but everything he tried, Evinrude simply swatted away.

Then Evinrude went on the attack, and in three moves, he had dashed Philip's sword from his hand. "That," he said dryly, "was the Suchet Maneuver. Perhaps you can learn about it in Hell." Then he raised his sword.

"Oh, no, not *again!*" said Constance, and threw herself between them. "Nobody is killing anyone!" She turned to Philip. "Look, buddy, you lost. Just go away, okay? Go off into exile or something. We can still work this out peacefully, all right?" She looked pleadingly from one to the other. "Everyone gets to go home, okay?"

It almost worked. Philip was so stunned by his unexpected loss that he might actually have gone away into exile. Even Evinrude hesitated. "Well…" he said. "I suppose…"

Had Philip not said anything, things might have gone a very different way. But it is human nature to say something when one ought to remain quiet, and although as an angel Constance had great power, the one thing she could not do was predict when a human was going to open his mouth and ruin the moment. "Good," he said, "So I'll go back to Shirleyhold and keep Lydwin, and you can go back to your family home in Charmingfell, and between us we can work out who keeps the country, and -"

"What do you mean, keep Lydwin?" Evinrude said. "You stole Lydwin after you murdered Amaryllis and used her death to launch a war!"

"So?" Philip said. "I still won it in a fair fight. Is it my fault the Lydwinish can't defend their own kingdom?"

"Now hang on-" Constance tried to cut in. In doing so she turned her back on Evinrude. This was a mistake. Evinrude used no clever swordplay, no classic technique or swashbuckling maneuver this time. He threw his sword hard as he could, over Constance's shoulder right into Philip's head. Philip went down with a thud, and didn't move.

"Oh shoot," Constance said, "Now I have to resurrect him *again!*"

"And I'll keep killing him," Evinrude said. "He is my sworn enemy and deserves to die. Either he goes or I do."

"I'm not going to kill *you!*" Constance said in exasperation.

"Aren't you?" Evinrude said. "Then what are you going to do, angel?"

"Well…" Constance said, desperately stalling for time.

Then Eulalie stepped forward. "Excuse me," she said. "Perhaps you could ask what I think."

"What?" Evinrude said.

"Exactly," Eulalie said. "You used to care what I think. We corresponded, remember. Very long letters. I saved them all. They're still back in my room in the castle, or at least they should be. Maybe Philip absconded with them, I don't know. At any rate, we talked about a great many things. I thought you cared about me, and I was even willing to overlook the fact that you were more or less promised to someone else."

"I did care-" Evinrude started to say.

"But," Eulalie cut him off with raised hand. "I came back from Heaven to Loventry to be with you and save the country from Philip. But now I can't be with you. Not as you are. I don't know if you can turn back to good or not. But I will not marry you now. Not like this."

Lady Eulalie turned on her heel and walked away into the woods towards her island. Evinrude watched her go, thunderstruck. Constance, equally surprised, had enough presence of mind to resurrect Philip and then knock him unconscious just to preserve the status quo. "Right," she said to no one in particular. "Well, now what?"

Then soldiers emerged from the trees, accompanied by generals on horseback and an assortment of griffins. Evinrude gathered himself. "You're all under arrest, angels or not," he said.

"Wanna bet?" Constance said, and extended her wings. The three angels vanished, reappearing on the beach of Isle Turtledove, right on the scorch mark where Eulalie had first been flamed by the dragon. Constance looked around. "Oh no," she said, slapping a hand to her forehead. "I forgot Philip!"

Sure enough, back in the woods Philip was still lying on the ground. Evinrude stood over him, sword raised. After a long moment, he sighed and lowered the sword. "Well, arrest him at least anyway. He'll be tried for the murder of Lady Amaryllis later. There's no point in anything else now."

"Sir?" one of the generals said.

"Never mind," Evinrude said. "Just do it. And withdraw the soldiers from before Isle Turtledove. The war is over. Also, send messages to begin a withdrawal from Lydwin. They are to be restored to full sovereignty. We'll work out the rest diplomatically later."

"Yes, sir," the general said, and departed with a salute. Slowly, the army began to rumble into motion in the night. Evinrude looked up at the stars. Constance's words echoed in his mind. "So," he said to himself. "Now what, indeed?"

He pondered over it for a long while. Finally he shrugged. "I might as well be king," he said. "It is my right, after all. It's what I should've been."

Evinrude's fist clenched. The decision was made. Once he had the army sorted, he would go to Laffin and arrange for his coronation. Only then would he have done what he set out to do.

13: The Further Investigations of Peter

Inside the walls of Ilariana, all was usually quiet. The walls were sturdy and had never been breached in living memory, and so no one feared invasion. Ilariana's streets were well-patrolled by the local police, who were thorough in their duty and kept a sharp eye out for trouble. They prized Ilariana's reputation as a trading city and safe haven for travelers, and they came down hard on anyone who endangered that reputation.

The Mercenary Guild had fit uneasily into all this at first. As traditional mercenaries, they offered to do any number of clean and dirty jobs for anyone who could pay, including theft, burglary, and murder, along with more complex affairs involving political assassinations or military adventures. This hadn't gone over well with the Ilariana police force, who didn't appreciate their citizens or guests being murdered by mercenaries. There had been fierce squabbles that threatened to break into all-out war, until finally the police and the mercenaries had come to a reluctant agreement. The Mercenary Guild now handed over a certain sum of their profits to the police and declined jobs that involved overthrowing the city leadership, and in return the police and the city leaders politely looked the other way at whatever other jobs the Guild undertook. It was an arrangement that worked out well for everyone, except for the poor souls that got waylaid in the alleys after dark.

Peter the Rabbit wizard had not yet fallen prey to a mercenary. He had tried his best. He had loitered in the streets after sundown, he had lingered outside the seediest taverns he could find, he had even mussed up his hair and tried to look scruffy and down on his luck. Instead of attracting muggers or soldiers of fortune looking for a job, he had mostly drawn the attention of the sisters of the Charitable Order of the Fruitful Cactus. These helpful and well-meaning women had assumed he was a wayward mendicant and pressed upon him gifts of clothing and food, even insisting that he stay in one of their guest cottages. The Mother Superior was just about to offer him a job as a gardener when Peter reluctantly drew out his wand and revealed his identity. There was no little embarrassment all around, and Peter found himself assuaging the sisters' hurt feelings by donating rather generously from his own pocket to their fund for the truly poor and needy. Then he had departed swiftly from their grounds, feeling sure that he was not going to find the headquarters of the Mercenary Guild inside a convent.

After leaving the convent, Peter had checked the Ilariana papers, looked for advertisements, and made other inquiries, but had come up with nothing. Even the police force refused to discuss it. Evidently the Mercenary Guild operated its business entirely by word of mouth, except that nobody was talking about it, at least to Peter.

On the same night that Philip had been overthrown in Loventry, Peter had almost given up. He had taken a room in a modest inn close to the walls; now, as he looked out of his window, he sighed and reached for the sock in his pocket. Then he remembered that he ought to settle up his bill first. He checked his other pocket to make sure he had the funds to cover it; happily he did, just. The Rabbit Order was generous with travel expenses but not overly so.

Peter made his way downstairs to the bar and looked round for the innkeeper. He found the man quickly and settled up, then made his way outside the city. The guards gave him wary looks as he departed. People usually didn't set off from Ilariana after dark unless they were up to no good, or so the rumors went.

He made his way to the same sand dune in which he had first landed. The jackal that had confronted him was nowhere to be seen. Peter sighed in relief and reached for his sock. Then he heard an unmistakable hissing sound. "Of course," he said, "I go looking for a mercenary and I find a snake. It just figures."

"Ah," said the snake, pausing just as it was about to strike. "You are looking for the mercenaries?"

Peter blinked. "You can talk?"

"Of course," the snake said sibilantly. "All the snakes of Ilariana can speak. The Mercenary Guild uses us to set up its contacts. It's business-like."

"Oh," Peter said, "Well, that makes sense. Right, yes, I am looking for the Mercenary Guild, as a matter of fact. Can you take me there?"

The snake eyed Peter sideways. "What is your purpose, if I may ask?"

Peter thought about lying for a moment. On the one hand, he wasn't sure how the Mercenary Guild would take the idea of him showing up to investigate one of their own. On the other hand, his attempt at a cover story in Ilariana hadn't worked very well with the sisters of the Fruitful Cactus. Also, whatever else the wizards of the Order of the Rabbit were, they tried to be scrupulously honest in their dealings. It set them apart from other orders, particularly the Polecats.

"I want to know why one of your members was hired to kill a dragon on Kirtle Island," Peter said, "And then I'd like to know who killed him. Whoever it was probably murdered the Prime Minister of my country, Loventry, and the Prime Minister's father. I'd like to do something about that."

The snake hissed in surprise. "Are you serious?"

"Very," said Peter. ""May I speak with the Guild now?"

"Wait, please," the snake said, and slithered quickly away into the sands. Peter had a feeling it wouldn't be gone long.

He was wrong about that, in a sense. The snake did not return. Instead, within an hour and just as Peter was beginning to get nervous, an armed squad of a dozen mercenaries emerged like wraiths from the sand and surrounded him. "Come with us," one said brusquely, a dull scimitar in his hand.

"I'd like nothing better," Peter replied, and calmly put his wand away to show he meant no harm. The men did not seem impressed. They formed up around him, making sure he would not escape.

Then the man with the scimitar spoke again. "Hand over your socks."

"I beg your pardon?" Peter said, trying to sound offended. Inside, however, he was rather alarmed. He had thought the Sock Dimension was a closely held secret inside the wizard orders. The

Mercenary Guild was exceptionally well informed if they knew about that.

"You heard me," the man said. "Both of them. And any in your pockets. Right now, or you won't find out what you came for. Also you'll die."

"Very well," Peter said reluctantly. The dying part didn't scare him as much; he was reasonably sure he could defend himself in a scrap if it came to that. What decided him was the mercenary's threat to withdraw and prevent him from getting his answers. These men were certainly competent, and no mistake. With a sigh, he pulled off his boots and removed his socks, then handed over the spare sock he kept in his pocket for travel purposes. They patted him down thoroughly just to be sure.

"Good," the leader said, once he was satisfied. "Now follow me." They turned and started down the road, Peter in the middle. He soon realized that they were headed right for the clump of palm trees he had slept next to on his first night in Ilariana. "Your headquarters isn't there, is it?" he said in disbelief.

"You'll see," the leader said as they neared the palm trees. They stopped at the brink of the pool around which the trees clustered. The leader checked to make sure no one was nearby as the mercenaries with him deployed to ensure it stayed that way. Then he strode to a particular tree and did something to a spot on the bark Peter didn't quite see. The next thing Peter knew there was a sudden, almost familiar cloth-like blur and a flashing forward, and then he was standing on a cool stone platform while the pool waters flowed peacefully over his head. Around him, in a dim stone chamber lit by flickering blue lights, several corridors branched away in different directions. Next to Peter, the mercenary leader calmly slipped a small soft object into his pocket. Peter recognized it at once. ""You've got access to-" he began, shocked.

"Yeah, something like," the leader said. "Favor from a friend."

"How?" Peter asked.

"Do you honestly expect me to tell you?" the man said, before escorting Peter down one of the corridors. It took several different twists and turns before depositing Peter in a room with a single table and a few chairs. "Wait here," the man said, before turning and closing the door. Peter duly waited.

Some time passed. Peter drummed his fingers on the table and waited a bit more. At last the door opened, and a harried man in a rumpled brown cloak pushed through, carrying a sheaf of papers. "All right," he said, adjusting his glasses and staring at Peter, "Now I don't have much time, we're involved in so much these days, you've no idea. My name is Barnes, Mercenary Guild Leader, and you're Peter, Order of the Rabbit, right? Making inquiries about our man in Kirtle Island?"

"Yes," Peter said, "That's me. I want to know why-"

"Right, right," Barnes said impatiently, cutting him off with a wave. "Cecil told us all that."

"Cecil?"

"The snake. One of our most trusted."

"Ah," Peter said.

"Well, anyway, here's the thing," Barnes said, setting down the papers on the table and looking Peter squarely in the eye for the first time. "Normally I couldn't tell you much. Nothing at all, really. Actually I'd have to kill you; we do take our work seriously around here, you know. Confidentiality and all that. However..." he said, as he noticed Peter's hand edging towards his wand.

"However," Barnes continued, "We also take seriously one of our own being murdered. It's one of our few absolute requirements. We'll generally do whatever job we're paid for, and it's one thing if one of us is killed in the course of duty, fighting in a battle or a duel, but if one of us is killed deliberately, targeted as it were, well, that's another thing altogether. So, in short, I will answer your questions about this matter."

"I see," Peter said. He took a breath, not having expected Barnes to actually be willing to answer him. "Well, then, ah..."

"Why don't I give you a start?" Barnes said kindly. "First, you wanted to know why our man was hired to kill a dragon on Kirtle Island. His name was Williams, by the way. Our man, not the dragon. Well, you must understand that we don't normally inquire about motives. It's not good for business, you know."

Peter felt at sea again. "But-"

"However," Barnes said. "In this case, the dragon-slaying was explained to us as part of a somewhat intricate scheme. I won't go through the whole affair, but the point of it all was to draw in a certain wizard, Mortimer, who belonged to the Order of the Polecat, get him to reveal his identity, and ensure that Mortimer would be murdered. I assume you're aware of who Mortimer is?"

"Oh yes," Peter said grimly, "I know. Rowena's father. Which leads me to my next question, I suppose. Who killed her?"

"Ah," Barnes said, "Well, we've done a little investigative work ourselves, on the quiet. When Williams didn't send in his last report, we grew alarmed and began to look into the matter. We keep track of our people, you know." He said this almost defensively, as if he expected Peter to accuse him of not keeping track of the mercenaries. Peter of course hadn't been thinking anything of the sort.

"First," Barnes went on, "we found that Williams was killed by magic. There wasn't a wound on him, and the only mark looked like this." He drew out a paper and pointed to a symbol traced carefully on it. Peter recognized the standard death curse at once.

"We know you Rabbit wizards don't use this, not usually, so it must have been a Polecat," Barnes said, "or a wizard of another order gone very bad. Then we heard stories of the Prime Minister killing off sailors on a ship near St. Alexander, and we put two and two together."

"So…" Peter said, trying to put things together himself, "Williams killed Mortimer, and Rowena killed Williams. So then…"

"Who killed Rowena? Well, that's where the circle closes," Barnes said, "We believe it's the same person that hired Williams. One of our people made a few inquiries, and a servant's uniform went missing on the night of the banquet at Lord Ryan's castle when Rowena was poisoned. Additionally, the poison that was used was a particular kind; we were, after some doing, able to retrieve a remnant of it."

Peter delicately didn't ask how the mercenaries had retrieved poison from a dead wizard's body. Barnes withdrew another paper. "It was made," he said, "from dragon venom."

"Really," Peter said. "I'm not sure I understand what that proves."

"Well, as it happened, we also had a bit of the venom from the dragon that was killed on Kirtle Island, before you disintegrated it," Barnes said. "Williams had the foresight to gather some before he was murdered. We found it in his possessions, and compared that with the venom that killed Rowena. It matched. And so it all ties together, you see. I'll save you the rest of our investigations, the letters we found, and so on, but it all points to one man, the man who hired Williams in the first place. This man, we've found, was in love with Lady Eulalie, and had reason to want vengeance on those who killed her."

Peter waited. Barnes clearly wanted him to ask the obvious "Who?" but when Peter didn't, he finally gave up and said it. "Prince Evinrude of House Charming," he said.

"Oh," Peter said. He hadn't expected that at all. "Are you sure?" It was an obvious question, but this time he couldn't help it. He, like almost everyone else in Loventry, had been pretty certain Evinrude was dead.

Barnes smiled and produced a final paper. "Whenever a mercenary is hired, a contract is signed and filed with us here in Ilariana. Another inviolable principle. We keep it confidential, of course, but we do require payment and a proper signature, a true name, confirmed by a notary magic. You understand why."

"Of course," Peter said. He looked down at the contract. It was sealed and done in correct legal terms, and signed, sure enough, in the flowing cursive of Prince Evinrude himself. "That's proof enough," he said. "But why?"

"As I said, it all ties together," Barnes said. "Mortimer summoned the dragon that killed Lady Eulalie. Mortimer was hired by Philip of House Shirley, who arranged Eulalie's murder so he could become king of Loventry. Rowena supported him in return for becoming the Prime Minister, which she wanted to ensure the truth would not be revealed about her Polecat father. Evinrude found out about it all and wanted vengeance."

"Oh," Peter said, taking it in. "But Evinrude is dead, isn't he? I thought he went off in search of the dragon weeks ago and no one's seen him since. Could someone have forged his signature?"

"It's just possible, but then again, he is definitely alive," Barnes said. "He's been quite active too. One of our people spotted him just recently in Loventry near Isle Turtledove just a few days ago."

"Ah," Peter said. "I see."

"Indeed," Barnes said. "I trust that answers your inquiries?"

"It does," Peter said. He looked down at the contract. "May I borrow this?"

"Of course," Barnes said. "Evinrude is now likely to become the king of Loventry, and I'm sure your Rabbit Council will want to address that. If you should require our assistance…"

"I'll let them know," Peter said delicately, rising from his chair. He didn't want to commit to anything more than that, for obvious reasons.

"Do that," Barnes said, also rising. "We'll escort you outside to the oasis. I assume you can find your way back from there?"

"I can," Peter said. He sighed, hating to have to address the obvious. "If you'll give me back my socks?"

"Of course," Barnes said, with just the hint of a smile.

With the incriminating contract in hand, his socks returned to him, Peter was quickly escorted out of the Mercenary Guild headquarters and deposited back at the pool by the palm trees. The mercenaries did not hang around for fond farewells but quickly disappeared. Peter, almost certain they were still watching him, reached for the spare sock which he had carefully stowed away in his pocket again. He muttered the words, wondering if the mercenaries knew those too. They really did seem remarkably well informed. When all this business was over, Peter decided he might say a word or two to the Council about that.

The oasis swirled away in a blur of fuzz around him. Soon the blur spun back again into St. Alexander, in Peter's own room, specifically. He took a moment to take in the comforts of home, and then took up his magic mirror and tried to get it to work once more. He had a lot to say to the Rabbit High Council, and he had a distinct feeling he had not much time in which to say it.

14: Coronation

On Isle Turtledove, things settled into an odd sort of stalemate. The army on the shore went home, dragons, griffins, and all. Evinrude sent a cautious emissary over to Lady Eulalie asking for a meeting. She refused point-blank. Gilbert delicately suggested she reconsider in the interests of peace.

"I'm actually with him on this one," Constance said. "I mean, if you guys don't get back together and settle things, what was the point?"

"No," said Lady Eulalie, and that had been that. Not even Sally could dissuade her. The poor angel tried her best, but to no avail. Eulalie set herself hard against any meeting whatsoever with Evinrude. She instead went about seeing to her island's affairs, making sure its supplies and defenses were in order, and to all appearances looking like she was preparing for another attack.

This upset Sally very much. "What am I supposed to do?" she exclaimed to Constance one evening a week after the overthrow of Philip. "I thought all of this was supposed to end happily!"

"Not everything has a happy ending," Constance said. "I met an angel, Tabitha, a little while back. You should talk to her sometime. She was in charge of garden security way back in the beginning. Boy, has she got stories."

Meanwhile Evinrude set about trying to bring the kingdom to some semblance of order again. After making sure Philip's army was withdrawing from Lydwin and sending messages to arrange a peace with the rebel movement (there's always a rebel movement), he took steps to set up a proper coronation. The Loventry noble families cautiously lent their support, although Evinrude got the sense they were waiting for something. To that end, he sent messages to the various wizard orders to shore up their support. He left out the Polecats for obvious reasons.

Most of them supported him, as they didn't much like the Polecats either; the Rabbit Order, curiously, held back. They didn't quite say why, only that they weren't quite ready to make a full commitment. Evinrude shrugged. He was the rightful king, he knew that, and he knew that Philip had hired the dragon and murdered Eulalie. That seemed to be good enough for the other families and wizard orders. What else was there?

At any rate, he didn't see the Rabbit hesitancy as a reason to hold things up. And so, three weeks after the confrontation on the shore opposite Isle Turtledove, Loventry's noble families and a good deal of its common folk gathered in the Great Hall at Laffin for the coronation.

The general mood of the common folk was mild surprise. They hadn't kept up with the latest doings, being mostly concerned with their own affairs, although the ones who lived near Isle Turtledove and its environs had been much annoyed by all the dragons and soldiers running around. Everyone had been upset of course to hear that Eulalie had been flamed and then that Amaryllis had been murdered and Lydwin had done the murdering, and a little confused to learn that Philip was the new king. House Shirley was reasonably powerful, but not that powerful, so far as they knew. Also Evinrude should've been king, they had thought, but he seemed to have disappeared, and no one knew where. The confusion had mounted when word spread that Philip had laid siege to Isle Turtledove, which as far as people knew was still part of Loventry.

Then suddenly the tales had gone wild. No one knew quite for sure what had happened, except something had gone wrong for Philip's forces. Some people swore that angels had shown up; others said it was people from, well, they didn't like to say, but they would venture it certainly wasn't angels. The overall feeling was that it was definitely unusual.

Next thing they knew, Philip was under arrest, the army was dispersed, and Prince Evinrude was back and on his way to be king. And so the common folk had gathered at the capital, some hoping to see Evinrude, most hoping to see angels. One or two hoped to see the people from the other side out of a sense of morbid curiosity.

Constance was there too. Sally had stayed on Isle Turtledove to keep an eye on things there, but Constance and Gilbert had traveled to see the coronation. "I wish I could do it," Constance said, as the two angels stood invisibly at the back of the Great Hall. Her fingers twitched ever so slightly as she saw the gleam of the richly ornamented crown in the Archbishop's hands. "You know. Just for fun."

"I'm told we can't," Gilbert said. "It's better if the humans crown themselves. If you show yourself and crown him, then you give his family a political advantage over the others, a sort of divine endorsement, and one never knows where that will end up."

"Yeah, yeah," Constance sighed. "But still. It'd be fun. And we practically put him on the throne anyway."

"Yes…" Gilbert said uneasily. "There is that. Well, let's just hope the coronation goes all right, then I can get back to the duty, and you can get back to…whatever you were doing before."

"Bear cubs," Constance said. "It's been bear cubs lately. Bear cubs are fun. Although I've been thinking of bringing back puppies!"

Gilbert, a little confused, didn't press further. They watched as the ceremony continued. Choirs sang beautiful hymns, and the Archbishop delivered various and sundry prayers for God's blessings upon the new king. Constance thought about taking notes on the hymns to deliver back to the Angel Choir, but she decided against it. She had never been much for the Angel Choir anyway.

Then, finally, the big moment came. Silence fell in the Great Hall as Evinrude stepped forward and knelt in the sight of all the respectful crowd. The Archbishop lifted the heavy crown high so everyone could see. Then, after a slight pause for effect, he prepared to lower it.

"Evinrude," said the Archbishop, "Prince of House Charming, Lord of Charmingfell, by the grace of God I crown you King of Loven-"

"Stop!" a voice boomed across the Great Hall. A bolt of yellow light flashed through the air, and to everyone's surprise (most of all the Archbishop's) the crown vanished completely from his hands. "Oh blast," said the voice. "I meant to turn it into doves."

Evinrude leapt to his feet, drawing the ceremonial sword he carried, which fortunately was just as sharp as an ordinary sword. At the rear of the Great Hall, just inside the massive entrance doors, stood a line of wizards in brown Rabbit robes. At their head was Egmond, his full white beard fairly bristling with fury. Peter flanked him nervously on his left. He would've preferred a less dramatic move, to be honest, but Egmond had insisted.

"Evinrude," Egmond thundered, "You are not fit to wear the crown of Loventry! You are no true king! I, Egmond, Leader of the High Council of the Order of the Rabbit, accuse you of the murder of Prime Minister Rowena!"

The crowd gasped. Even the Archbishop looked astonished. "Oh boy," Constance said.

"And this," Gilbert said quietly, "is why we don't like to interfere. It never goes right, somehow. Just once I wish it would. But it never does."

Everyone waited for the Crown Prince to deny the accusation, or perhaps to challenge Egmond to a duel. Instead, Evinrude almost smiled. "Yes," he said calmly. "I did, actually. I used dragon venom. I got it from the dragon that was used to murder Lady Eulalie of Isle Turtledove. That I didn't do; King Philip did that. Rowena was in league with him; did you know?"

Egmond paused. The pause was just long enough for everyone watching to realize that he very much did know. "I see," Evinrude said. "So what now? Will you arrest me for the supposed crime of vengeance upon the woman in league with the assassin of Lady Eulalie? Especially when you know that Rowena was working with him? Are you going to let Philip take the throne? Or will you back down and allow the coronation to continue as it should have done long before all this?"

The wizard looked down at his wand, then back up at the Crown Prince. He couldn't just allow Evinrude to get away with the murder of a wizard and a prime minister, even if she had chosen her alliances badly. On the other hand, Egmond had interrupted the coronation;

he couldn't very well say "I'm sorry, never mind," and walk away. It was a stalemate, and he had no idea how to break it.

Gilbert, at the back, sighed. He missed doing the duty back on Earth. Cleaning up after an ordinary death was so much tidier. "All right," he said to Constance. "I suppose you had better do something."

Constance didn't say anything, for the simple reason that she wasn't there. Gilbert turned in alarm, but the angel wasn't beside him. He shot a glance around the Great Hall, but he couldn't see her anywhere around. Then, suddenly, the doors beside him banged open, and Constance marched through. Beside her was a very upset Lady Eulalie. "I have had enough of this!" Eulalie announced. "Enough! I am going to be queen of Loventry, and that settles that!"

"Excuse me?" Evinrude said.

"I haven't murdered anyone," Eulalie said, "and I'm not in league with anyone who has. So between you, Philip, and me, who do you think is the best choice?"

"You have a point," Egmond said, vastly relieved to see a way out of his dilemma.

"I agree," Peter said quickly.

"Well, I don't!" Evinrude said furiously, raising his ceremonial sword. "I have the right to the crown, it's mine! If you're going to challenge me-"

"You'll what?" Eulalie said, with only the slightest tremor in her voice. "Arrest me? Kill me? You seem to be doing that a lot of late, Evinrude. I thought, after we met last time, you might have changed. I hoped that maybe you might have turned back to good. But now I see that you haven't."

"So what are you going to do?" Evinrude said, raising his ceremonial sword.

"I have an idea," Sally suggested, abruptly stepping forward. She had tailed along with Eulalie when Constance had shown up on the island and said that Eulalie was desperately needed at the capital. As it happened, long before she had become an angel, Sally had been a political science student. "How about you all try constitutional democracy?"

"What?" said Eulalie and Evinrude together. Constance smacked her palm against her face.

"Yeah!" Sally said enthusiastically. "See, it's a system where everybody gets together every so often and votes on who the leader's going to be! And also, it's not just voting, I mean, that's an important part of it, but another part of it is that you put down on paper what people's rights are so the government knows it can't take them away! It's fun! You should try it!"

"Let's return to that first bit," Evinrude said. "You said everyone gets together and…"

"Votes," Sally said. "They write down on paper who they choose to be the leader, and then their votes are counted, and the winner is the leader!" She realized she was oversimplifying things by a lot, but Sally figured this was a medieval society and she thought it best to start with the basics.

"Suppose they choose the wrong person?" Eulalie asked.

"Well," Sally began. "They can vote them out later!"

"And in the meantime?" Eulalie said. "What harm might they do to the country in the meantime? Also, who's counting the votes? Does that matter?"

"And who gets to vote?" Evinrude asked. "Does that include me? All Lords and Ladies? Them?" He gestured to the common folk, who perked up at the mention of this interesting new political system.

"Ah…" Sally said. She realized she might have underestimated Loventrian political savvy.

"Also, does Philip get a vote?" Evinrude said. "Because I will not let him be the king."

"There wouldn't *be* a king, really," Sally tried to explain. "Not in the absolute sense, I mean, you could have a constitutional monarchy, but you could also have a popularly elected executive officer or a parliament, there's all sorts of systems-"

"Wait a moment," Eulalie said. "I thought you said-"

"Enough!" Evinrude cut in. "We can discuss alternative political arrangements for Loventry on another day!" He turned to the Archbishop. "You. Crown me. Now."

Eulalie moved towards him. "No," she said, white-faced. "I won't allow it."

"And again," Evinrude said. "I ask, how are you going to stop me?"

"The only way I can," Eulalie said, and she looked around. There, in the crowd of common folk and nobility, she spotted someone she knew. "Lord Ryan," she said, "Can I borrow your sword?"

"Milady," Lord Ryan said, obviously embarrassed, "You cannot duel Prince Evinrude for the crown."

"Oh, can't I?" Eulalie said, bristling. "Is it because I am a woman?"

"No," Lord Ryan said, "It is because you literally cannot. We watched you grow up, remember. I don't recall you ever training in swordplay. Evinrude, on the other hand, is a master of the art. He would cut you down within five minutes."

"Four, probably," Evinrude interjected.

Lord Ryan turned a cold eye on him. "I would have a care, were I you; the only reason I don't take up the challenge on Lady Eulalie's behalf is that I'm hoping we can resolve this peacefully."

"Oh, really?" Evinrude said. "Perhaps you'd rather have the crown yourself!"

"Wait a minute," Eulalie began.

"Guys, this is getting out of hand," Constance said. "Also, did everyone forget that the wizard, what's his name, made the crown disappear anyway? Anyone?" She was ignored.

"I'm beginning to wonder if my taking the crown isn't the best idea," Lord Ryan said. "It's certainly better than having it go to you. I'm not so sure you're any better than Philip."

"I know of one way," Evinrude said. He raised his sword. Lord Ryan raised his. Before Eulalie or anyone else could stop them, the two men were at each other, swords flashing like steel lightning. This wasn't a duel like the one between Evinrude and Philip where only one man knew how to fight. This was a combat between masters, and it showed. If the thing hadn't been so serious, Constance might've considered selling tickets.

Gilbert felt a rustle of wings beside him. He turned, thinking Sally might've left, or that perhaps Constance really was selling tickets. To his surprise, it was another angel altogether. "Winifred?" Gilbert said. "What are you doing here?"

"I have the duty," Winifred said grimly. "This fight is to the death, you know."

Gilbert turned back. Lord Ryan and Evinrude were still going at it. At the moment he couldn't tell who was winning. "But-" he began. It hadn't quite occurred to him that one of the two men would die and that one of his colleagues would be called upon.

"And not just them," Winifred said. "There will be consequences, almost certainly a civil war. I expect Loventry will be tearing itself apart for decades to come."

"I did not expect…" Gilbert said, his voice trailing off.

"Did you ask?" Winifred said icily. "Or did you just follow Constance off on her adventure? You have to think about these things with Constance. I trained her and she's a good angel now, but she is a bit more…eccentric than some of us. Oh, look, Lord Ryan's down."

Sure enough, Lord Ryan had missed a step and Evinrude had done a swift kick that knocked him off balance. As he tried to regain it, his hold loosened just slightly on the hilt of his sword, and Evinrude was in with a quick slash that drove the sword from Lord Ryan's hand in a blow that left him wincing in pain. Next moment Lord Ryan was down on one knee and Evinrude's blade was at his throat. "Well?" Evinrude said, breathing hard.

"I…" Lord Ryan gasped, "I yield."

"Do you?" Evinrude said, not moving his sword. "And now I walk away and leave you with your castle and your lands and your knights, and you'll rise against me at the next opportunity, is that it? This all started because I couldn't keep my crown secure, because Philip challenged my right to the throne. How do I know you won't do the same?"

Lord Ryan looked taken aback. He clearly hadn't expected things to go this way. "I promise, I will not rise against you. I only challenged you now because of Lady Eulalie-"

"Yes, and she's still there, and so how can I believe you?" Evinrude shot back. "No, there's really only one way to be sure, isn't there?" He raised his sword.

Then he dropped it, for the simple reason that he had just been struck in the head with a large heavy object. A loud *clonk* resounded through the Great Hall. Evinrude dropped to the floor. Lord Ryan blinked; he definitely hadn't expected that to happen either. He looked down at the object that had felled the unconscious Crown Prince. "Is this…" he said hesitantly, "a corset?"

"Erm, yes," Eulalie said, blushing. "Sorry. I'd like that back please. It's whalebone, you know, very rare. Mother made it. I'm just glad I had it on this time, I didn't when the dragon… but you didn't need to know that."

"How did you…" Lord Ryan began.

"I would rather not discuss it," she said, stepping forward so Lord Ryan could gingerly hand her back her corset. "All I'll say is that it was very tricky work. I got it off just in time."

"Ah," Lord Ryan said. The crowd of common folk, courtiers, and Rabbit wizards looked about in a sort of general embarrassment. Peter coughed nervously; the cough resounded in the Great Hall, which had wonderful acoustics.

"Excuse me," the Archbishop said plaintively. "What do I do about the crowning then?" He gestured vaguely at the air. Egmond sighed and flicked his wand, and the crown rematerialized in the Archbishop's hands.

"Lord Ryan can have it," Eulalie said, waving it off. "I'm going back to Isle Turtledove." With that, she turned and marched out the door.

"Well then," Winifred said, watching her depart. "I suppose I'm not needed after all."

"Guess not," Constance said, giggling. "Corset-punch. That was hilarious. I gotta remember that!"

No one ventured to ask her whether angels wore corsets; the situation was awkward enough as it was.

"I wonder when Eulalie will realize she needs someone to fly her back?" Gilbert mused.

"Right about… now," Constance said. Sure enough, the door opened and Eulalie poked her head in.

"Ah, Sally? Constance? Anyone?"

"I'll do it!" Sally volunteered. "Everything's okay here now, right?"

"Yeah," Constance said, looking over at the unconscious Evinrude. "Everything's okay."

Lord Ryan of House Brendan was crowned king of Loventry in a somewhat more subdued ceremony the next day. After consultation with Egmond and Peter, he decided the best thing to do with Philip and Evinrude, rather than lock them up in a castle dungeon somewhere, was to send them into exile. "I don't care where you go," he said, "Though, Philip, I wouldn't recommend Lydwin. You're not very popular up there, as you can imagine. But never return here."

"Fine," Philip said. "You just wait. I will return someday, with an army of my own. You just wait!"

Evinrude said nothing. He continued to say nothing until Ryan's soldiers had deposited him at the border of Loventry, on the road that led towards Ilariana in the south. He had been given a full supply of provisions to tide him over till he reached the city. "What you do after that's your business, I'm told," the captain said. "I hear there's mercenaries there."

"I've heard that too," Evinrude said.

The soldiers left, and he was alone in the desert sun. Then a shadow appeared. "Leon. I was wondering when you would show up."

"I'm not allowed back in Loventry," Leon said. "The boss doesn't like that. Hates his people getting cast out of places. Really ticks him off. But hey, at least I get a bonus. A deal's a deal, right?"

"Right," said Evinrude.

There was a flash of fire, and then there was no one in the desert at all.

Lady Eulalie made it safely back to her island with the help of the angels. Sally actually cried; she was so happy. "Things went all right!" she said. "Everyone was saved!"

Gilbert was about to point out that they had lost Evinrude, but Constance elbowed him sharply and he shut up. "So," he said instead, "I suppose I shall go and take up the duty again."

"If you're ever in Loventry again, you must stop by," Lady Eulalie said. "What duty was that again?"

"It's… complicated," Gilbert said.

"Ah," Eulalie said, and left it at that.

The three angels stood on the scorch mark where Eulalie had been flamed by the dragon, and, as a last favor, Constance snapped it away, leaving golden sand behind. "Well, back to Heaven, then," said Constance. "See you around, guys!"

"Yes," said Gilbert, "Quite."

"Bye!" Sally said. They disappeared in a spray of light. Lady Eulalie watched them go. Then, with a sigh, she went back into the castle, and slipped into the chapel. She still had a lot she wanted to do, but first, she wanted to take a moment before the day's work began. And so, Lady Eulalie bowed her head and prayed for the soul of Prince Evinrude as the sun rose outside, dimming out the stars.

Meanwhile, far across the sea from Isle Turtledove, something was stirring beneath the waves. What Constance, Sally, and everyone else had forgotten about was that Evinrude's quest for vengeance had an unforeseen consequence. Rowena's detour had caused Evinrude to stumble into awakening an ancient evil, a monster that had slept on his island for centuries undisturbed. Now the giant was awake. He'd had his morning snack, namely Evinrude, and had gone back to sleep for a bit, but now he was awake again. And, as one usually is, he was still hungry. Grendel was on the move. Worse, he wanted his mother.

Michael S. Atkinson

Acknowledgments

First, the credit for this sequel must once again in large part go to my wife Nicole, who once again created the cover art and edited the story; any remaining edits are, as before, my own.

I should also thank the people at the Trifecta writing challenge, a regular writing prompt site that closed up in 2014, and for whom I first wrote the stories which eventually evolved into this work. Once again I drew inspiration from Dante Alighieri's *Divine Comedy*, this time the *Purgatorio* section. I also should thank the people responsible for the old Disney movie *The Rescuers,* mostly because I always wanted to name someone Evinrude. Any resemblance between my Evinrude and the little insect in the movie is entirely coincidental.